IN THE FAR LANDS

(A STORY)

O. HULDUMANN

ISBN: 9798674733935

Copyright © 2019 O. Huldumann

The moral right of the author has been asserted in accordance with Section 77 of the Copyright, Designs and Patents Act 1988.

All rights reserved. No part of this publication may be reproduced, stored in a retrieval system, or transmitted, in any form, or by any means, without prior permission in writing.

For RJW, SP and – DOY – CC

I DO NOT KNOW what I may appear to the world, but to myself I seem to have been only like a boy playing on the sea-shore, and diverting myself in now and then finding a smoother pebble or a prettier shell than ordinary, whilst the great ocean of truth lay all undiscovered before me.

Isaac Newton

IN THE FAR LANDS

✳

ISSY

FOR THE BEST

In the Far Lands, the is-Lands (because it is land), they come to us. Not often now, it's true, but often enough that we know there is still somewhere to come *from*, though we do not wish to go there or know there.

So we ask them not to speak of it – that somewhere – and they do not. That is the Rule. And most who come would not want to speak of it anyway, because it is far behind them and if it wasn't they wouldn't be here. So it isn't spoken of and that's for the best.

Nor do we ask why they have come, because that is obvious. Sometimes it is obvious from what they bring with them: the things they valued the most and could not leave.

(I have seen them arrive with nothing more than a small porcelain cat; curled, wrapped in brown paper, tied with a string, no larger than an egg – smaller in fact. And I have seen them arrive with large leather suitcases – bound by sturdy leather straps with brass buckles – so heavy that they require two hands to lift. They are weighed down by the knowing that this wasn't all they wanted to bring. The boats are never large, though. That is the way. It's for the best.)

Sometimes why they have come is obvious from their faces.

I liked the man with the porcelain cat when he arrived because all he wanted to bring was the cat. Cats are welcome. Dogs are not.

THE SIISTERS

When there is to be an Arrival the Siisters will tell someone. We do not know if they *are* sisters and they do not look alike. But they act like sisters and that's enough.

Their names are Elaine and Simone and they spend all day in their tea room. It is called the Flying Horse Tea Room and it is in the basement of the Very Tall House Near The Square. To reach the tea room you must pass the spiked black railings – which prevent unwary pedestrians from falling down – and open the heavy wrought iron gate at the top of the granite steps – twelve.

That gate will snap at your hand. It has a way of biting your fingers. It is the reason that the Flying Horse Tea Room does not have more people coming down the steps to drink tea and eat cakes or have scrambled eggs on buttered toast.

Many people would like to go down to eat the things the Siisters prepare and some will look longingly through the railings for a glimpse of what is in the window, though it's hard to see. But many people do not trust that gate. They do not want their fingers bitten. So for most of the time the Siisters do not have many customers – perhaps one or two together – and sometimes they snooze and dream of new cakes to make.

They will also dream of when there will be an Arrival and whether it will be a good thing or not for people to gather and say hello and shake hands. The Siisters will tell someone about the Arrival and that person will leave the tea room and pass on the information. They will tell the Meyer where the incomers will arrive and what sort of reception they would appreciate, and by whom.

We may have a big parade and the brass band may play below fluttering bunting at the harbour side. Or the newcomers may be greeted by one person in a windswept coat standing by the high-water mark on a beach.

Whichever it is – or somewhere in between – the incomers will be met and there will be talk for a while – but not too long because we know their journey will have been tiring – and then they will be told where they may stay. Then they will leave their boat and take their porcelain cat or their large suitcase or something in between and be guided to their new accommodation.

I have only guided three people since I reached my Majority and was adopted (which is the Rule before you may attend an Arrival).

Each time I've said: "I'm Issy, which is short for Isadora. How do you do?"

There will be an Arrival soon.

AN ARRIVAL

It was half-morning and I was trying to collect a cloud-face which looked like an enormous man's head with a quiff and a hook chin. He was blowing out his cheeks to expel a second, smaller and more wispy cloud from his lips. The sky was a very clear light blue around the clouds and the sun was bright.

I had an egg in my hand and I was half way back from the chicken coop when I'd stopped to collect the cloud-face, but it was already changing and I knew I didn't have time to collect it properly, so I simply watched it until it was no longer the enormous head and that was when the Meyer arrived. He knew what I was looking at.

"That was a good one, ey?" he said. "Too bad we didn't have it for longer."

"Yes," I agreed.

"There's going to be an Arrival," he told me then, which I knew because he had come to find me. Usually I would just meet him on a street or a lane and say "Hello Charlie, Mr Meyer."

"I think they would like you to be there," the Meyer said. "There will be three. I have asked Francis Daychild and Marianna Klos to be there as well. I think that will be enough."

"I'll be happy to go," I told him. "This will be my fourth. Where will they Arrive?"

"At Silvermine Cove. It will be some time after midday."

"I'll be there by then," I said.

The Meyer, whose name is Charlie, nodded and said: "Good. Thank you, Issy. – Have you moved yet?"

"Nearly," I said. "Elaine and Simone will let me have the room at the top of their house. I think I'll like it there. I just need to tell my parents. I was going to do that this afternoon but I'll wait until after the Arrival now."

"Are you sure? I don't want the Arrival to be an imposition," Charlie said.

"Not at all. I'll like it," I told him.

"Oh. Good. Thank you," he said again.

SKY BLUE

When the Meyer had gone I took the egg in to Elaine who was in the kitchen.

"Only one," I showed her.

"Damn birds," she said.

The egg had become light blue in my hand, the same colour as the sky.

NO SILVER MINE

There is no silver mine at Silvermine Cove. There might have been one, once a once a time, but no-one has found it although people still look when they have nothing better to do. Then they will go out to Silvermine Cove and spend half a day treading through the brambles and the bracken and thickets on the land above the beach. In the end they always say *"There's no silver mine here. Someone's having us on."*

But they never mind too much because it is a pleasant way to spend an afternoon or a morning as long as you don't get scratched by too many brambles.

HOW ARE THE TREES?

I didn't want to be late for the Arrival. Silvermine Cove is on the far side of Faer is-Land so I left the Siisters to their baking in the kitchen before midday. Simone gave me a sandwich she had made with the sky-blue egg so that I would have something to eat.

To get to Silvermine Cove you must take the path as if you're going to Whelme is-Land; out past the Bardith Farm with the wheat ripening in the fields. There you may wave at the farmhouse as you pass and someone may wave back.

Past the farm I took the path which isn't the path to Whelme but which meanders towards Silvermine Cove. After I'd been walking for half an hour I decided it would be nice to eat against the stile, so that is what I did. I also had a bottle of lime drink and I drank that with the sky-blue egg sandwich. That was when Marianna arrived. She had come from Whelme so I knew that Charlie, Mr Meyer, had had a busy morning making sure we knew about the Arrival.

"Hello, Issy," Marianna said when she climbed the stile and came down next to me. "I hope we're not late."

"I don't think so," I said. She had on a skirt which swished the grass just above her ankles. "I'm not sure it's possible to be late for an Arrival. Only early."

"You might be right," she said. "I've sometimes thought that, too."

Because I'd finished eating my sandwich we walked on together.

"How are the trees?" I asked.

"Don't ask," Marianna said. "I've had trouble with them. They don't like some of my shapes, but I'm sure it's just a matter of persuading them that I know what I'm doing."

"I expect so," I said. "What sort are you using?"

"Mostly maple."

"I've heard they can be difficult," I said. "But I don't know who told me."

There is a broad sloping field above Silvermine Cove. It is rocky and overgrown because it is too steep and uneven to be much use for growing crops. That is where people go to look for the silver mine.

Beside this slope there is a rutted track which sinks down below the level of the surrounding land so that only your head is visible to anyone out on the field. Then your head disappears as the brambles and saplings grow up on either side of the track. It is a hidden, hollow way.

At the end of the track you emerge at a wooden gate with moss on its cross-members. Beyond this is a sandy path which leads around the entire island if you care to follow it. When you cross the path there is a set of wooden steps down to a broad, hard-sand beach.

Francis Daychild was already there.

Francis Daychild was old and scrawny. He looked like an old buzzard, if an old buzzard would wear a wool coat and a shirt collar too big for his neck which had a bobbing Adam's apple. I didn't know him well because he lived on Hallows and kept himself to himself. But as luck would have it he had been visiting his friend Irene near the Square that morning and that is where the Meyer ran into him and asked him if he would go to the Arrival.

"Hello, Francis," Marianna said as we approached him. He was sitting on a smooth, round rock where he could look out to sea.

"You're just in time," he told us.

THE BOAT

We could see the boat on the wide green sea. It had a single sail – a triangle of dark red, faded and salt stained, fraying at the edges.

I stood with Marianna and watched. Francis remained on his rock.

After a short time the boat changed course and headed for the beach with the warm wind behind its sail. It came to the centre of the beach where there are no rocks and nuzzled up to the sand.

Marianna and I hitched up our skirts and waded into the knee-deep water and took hold of the painter so that we could haul the boat on to the sand a little way. The boat looked as if it had been through a storm. There was a good amount of water slopping around over its ribs on the inside and the things the people had brought were wet and so were the people. When I looked more closely I could see that one of the clinkers had sprung from its nails. It made a hole the size of a mouth.

When the boat was as far on to the sand as we could get it we stood back and waited. The woman who sat on the plank across the centre of the boat looked at us anxiously, her face etched with worry.

"Are we there?" she said.

"I think so," the man said. "I don't think we can go any further."

He looked at us. He had steel-rimmed spectacles which made his eyes look soft and patient in a way which led you to think that he would be good at waiting because he would not give up no matter how long it took.

The boy was sitting in the bow and I wished he had moved back because his weight had made the boat harder to pull up on the sand. He was wearing a mackintosh and around his neck he had a small canvas bag on a canvas strap. It looked as if it might contain a book. I guessed it would be a storybook because of his age.

They looked at us in the same way that you look at the shape of a horse at the far end of a field when you know that it can't be a horse but that it must be something else. It takes you a while to shake off the shape of the horse and realise that it is a curved branch of a tree and the pattern of sunlight falling on a stone wall. That is when it becomes clear.

When we became clear the man said: "Can you tell us? Are we there?"

"Yes," Marianna said. "You've arrived. Do you want to step out of the boat?"

They did and they did. The man came first, offering a hand to help the woman, bringing her through the shallow water to the hard sand beyond the wave lap. Then he went back with the intention of helping the boy.

When the boy saw this he got out of the boat on his own and splashed to the shore, so the man reached in to the boat and lifted a canvas seaman's kitbag and a small cardboard suitcase with a metal handle. He brought them up on to the beach and placed them on the sand. They would need time to dry.

By now Francis Daychild had left his rock and come to stand at the line of dried seaweed. "We must tell you the Rule," Francis said.

THE RULE, & AFTERWARDS THE BOAT AGAIN

Francis told them the Rule in his cracked, scrawny voice which wasn't unpleasant to listen to.

It didn't take long. It doesn't take long to ask people not to do something they probably don't want to do anyway, at least not yet. Later, if they do feel that they want to do it, they also know why it would not be a good idea, so they do not mention it. It's for the best.

It takes less time to tell the Rule than to write this.

While Francis said his piece they all listened politely. Then Marianna said: "We have traditions and customs but you'll soon learn what they are. No-one will think the worse of you because you don't know them yet."

The man nodded. "Thank you," he said. Then he told us their names. His name was Martin. His wife was Dot and the boy was Patrice. We told them our names. I said: "I'm Issy. It's short for Isadora."

Dot and Patrice did not speak but we knew they were tired and had come a long way.

"I'll take you to Wendell's Place," Marianna told them. "He'll be expecting you now. If you'd like to follow me?"

So they picked up their bags. The man carried the kitbag. His wife carried the small suitcase. They followed us in a line towards the steps off the beach.

"What about the boat?" one of them said. It was probably Martin.

"Don't worry about the boat; it'll take care of itself," Marianna said. 'It'll find its own way home. If boats *have* a home. I don't know that they do."

At the top of the steps Marianna said she would take the incomers to Wendell's Place along the shore path. She thought it would be less tiring. It was on her way back to Whelme, too. I said I would go with them but she said it wasn't necessary, particularly as I wanted to speak to my parents that afternoon. So Francis and I watched as they went off along the shore path.

"That boat," Francis said. "Looked like it could use a lick of paint." He cast a glance back towards the beach.

"It needs more than a lick," I said. "It has a hole in it the size of a mouth."

He nodded. "Maybe I'll go get my paint," he said.

(By the time Francis returned some time later with his pots of paint and stiff brushes the boat had slipped away. "Oh well," he said. "Perhaps it didn't want to be painted. I suppose it knows what it's doing.")

THE WAITING ROOM

When I left Francis I set off to Fryst. When I went downhill I whistled through my teeth because I was glad the Arrival had gone well.

The bridge to Fryst is only accessible at the low tide. That is because whoever built that bridge did not build it high enough. Or perhaps they built it when the sea did not rise as far as it does now. Perhaps we should give them the benefit of the doubt.

When you cross the bridge you can look down into the clear water and see the deep water-valley and the span of the stone arches which support the path you're walking on. The path is only four feet wide and you cannot get a blade of grass between the stones. The arches beneath are very tall and slender and it is impossible to see how far they go down.

But before you reach the bridge you must pass a wooden shed on a small mound. This is the Waiting Room. It has a veranda with two cane chairs where you can sit and look out over the strait. Or you can sit inside behind the windows if the wind is cold from Fryst.

I went into the Waiting Room to retrieve my coat and boots. They were on the peg where I had left them. Of course they were. It is a sensible arrangement. No-one wants to leave Fryst and walk around all day in a heavy coat and boots. You would boil. So the Waiting Room is there to store your coat and boots until you return. They may remain there for as long as you like. It's up to you.

There was only one other coat hanging in the shed. Beneath it was a pair of thick leather boots so I knew only one other Frystian was not on the is-land.

At the far end of the Waiting Room, facing the door, there is a clock with one hand. It was made by Per si-Lversum. I know this because it feels like him and he is a deep, slow-stirring man, like the currents of the tide.

The clock hand does not move. Instead it is the face which turns, slowly, telling the height of the tide so that you can see how long you must wait before you can cross the bridge, or that you would have been in time to cross if you hadn't stopped to talk about moths and butterflies with someone on the way here, but now it is too late and you must wait.

I wound the clock with its square brass key which hangs on a rusty nail to the left. It is a custom to wind the clock when you use the waiting room, even if you don't wait. I had timed it right. It would be low tide in just a few moments so I didn't need to wait.

FRYST IS-LAND

The is-land is called Fryst because it is Winter there. To say the name properly you should say it like the sound of hard, dry snow blown against the side of a corrugated iron shack in the dark. That is how it is said.

I knew this was the sort of thing that Martin and Dot and Patrice would be told, perhaps by Wendell. They might have been talking about it right then, but I didn't think so. I didn't think that they would be talking much at all yet. Most incomers don't talk a lot to begin with. The smart ones listen.

Once you have gone over the Fryst bridge there is a single track which crosses the island to the far side in a straight line. It is worn into two ruts which are deep and often filled with melt-water. This is where you can find ice lizards when the water freezes. The ruts are made by the wheels of handcarts which bring wood and other necessities to the island. Each home has a handcart. No-one wants to walk back and forth in the snow and ice more than is necessary which is why the carts are useful.

There are good winter days and bad winter days on Fryst but all days are winter days.

A good winter day will be so clear and bright that you cannot look across the landscape without snow goggles. The sun will be as warm as a Whelme day and you will hear the chuckling sound of melt water under the ice-crust and the icicles will drip drip drip. You will look at the birch trees and admire how slender they are. On a good winter day you will wonder how you could ever leave this place.

A bad winter day will be the exact opposite of all I just said. There will be no sun and the snow will be stinging-hard and powdery in the wind. The temperature will be minus f and will shatter nails in their wood holes. It can stay that way for a week or more and you will wonder how you could ever leave this place.

Today was somewhere between the two and I knew how I would be leaving.

ICE LIZARDS

The straight track will take you to the far side of the island but before it gets there you reach the cross roads. The first part of the track between the bridge and the crossroads is narrow because it has dry-stone walls on either side. This is where you will find most ice lizards if you are good at spotting them.

They live in the surface of the frozen melt-water in the ruts of the track. I collect them in the same way I collect cloud-faces but it is easier because they do not change as rapidly. They change very very slowly. Sometimes they will take days and you can see them forming and think "*by tomorrow that will be a really good ice lizard. I will come back then.*" Unless someone passes along the track with a hand-cart, of course. Then, when you return, the ice lizard will be gone. Perhaps part of it will remain but it won't be an ice lizard any more. Sometimes the snow will cover them in the night. It is all a matter of chance.

When I collect an ice lizard it comes to live in my ice lizard book. In my life I have collected 167 but I have seen many more. I do not collect every one I see. Some are better left un-collected because you can tell they will be happier. Some would be trouble.

I saw two ice lizards but I didn't collect them. One looked as if it might be ready tomorrow.

FRYST VILLAGE

At the crossroads you turn left if you wish to go to Fryst Village and not to one of the houses which are away from the village because their inhabitants prefer even greater isolation. There may be thirty of these. I haven't counted accurately.

When you turn off at the crossroads the track is broader and very roughly paved with stones. You pass into the wide scoop of the valley which is beautifully smooth as it slides down to the broad bay. There are no trees to spoil the smoothness. The moss and lichen are as soft as a bed and the rivulets trickle daintily between freezes and you can hop across them on stepping stones even though they are less than an inch deep.

There had been a small thaw while I was away but I could sense that it would not last much longer. In the entrance to the bay Skelldottir was half lost in cloud. The stack of this off-island is hundreds of feet high and is often lost in cloud. Around it the iceberglets nuzzled and bumped each other like kittens.

I hopped the rivulets and skipped on towards the bay. It would be dark soon. It was nearly late afternoon.

From a distance the houses of Fryst Village look like building bricks scattered on the bare rocky shore. The houses are brightly coloured: red, yellow and blue. Each is the same. Each has a square window below the point of the gable on the second floor. The window faces Skelldottir.

Beside each house there is a smaller guest house for incomers. Many of the guest houses are older than the houses they belong to. They are build of stone with very thick walls and sod roofs. They are warm and comfortable. In the first days the people of Fryst Village lived in these houses and guests would live with them. It was only later that the newer houses were built and the residents went to live in them. There was more privacy all round.

METANISMS

When I arrived my father was sitting at the table which is his work bench. He has the fire at his back when he works. I think this is the only place where I will talk about him in this story but perhaps I will be wrong.

"Hello, Issy," he said and he smiled. "I see you've come back."

"Hello," I said. "How are the metanisms coming along?"

"Oh, you know, pretty good, some of them. Pretty good. I'd like to finish this one before I talk to you properly. Would that be all right?"

I said that it would and when I said that he smiled again and went back to work while I sat in the low chair by the fire and warmed my feet.

My father makes small mechanisms from metal. He calls them metanisms. They do not do anything but they do it very intricately.

He has a small lathe which was red when it was new, but that was a long time ago. Most of the red has worn away and now the cast iron and carbon steel of it is a burnished, oiled grey where his hands have rubbed and tools have scraped.

He turns the brass and copper and steel on the lathe. Occasionally he will adjust the steam pressure by the valve which emerges from the floor on its grey metal pipe. The pipe goes hundreds of feet down into the earth.

There is a story that deep beneath the surface the is-lands are hollow and porous like a sponge. The story says that the sea seeps into the holes and is turned to steam by the heat of the earth down there. The steam builds up in large chambers beneath the is-lands and the pipes that have been sunk into the ground for many hundreds of feet let the steam emerge. If you are clever like my father you can get the steam to power your lathe.

When I'd warmed my feet for a while my father was still working so I went to see my mother in the bedroom.

She was lying on the tartan wool rug which is laid over the bed. In her frame she was smiling as she always smiles. She looked happy to see me. I told her about the ice lizard which might be ready tomorrow and I told her about the Arrival but not in much detail. I also told her I would make a meal for my father because I thought he would probably be hungry when he finished the latest metanism. My mother seemed to agree.

LARGER THINGS

For a while my father thought he wanted to make larger things. He built a big lathe in the shed which was powered by wide belts which hummed and slapped. It took him months. It was a labour in itself.

When it was finished and working the way he wanted it to he made several large dish things on this lathe. He made them by pulling a polished bar against a spinning disc of metal and forming it to a wooden form, which he had also made. He made perfect hemispheres and burnished them, but in the end he stopped because the large dish things weren't what he was seeking. The big lathe is dusty and rusting now. The firewood is stacked around it.

When I had cooked the meal, which was a rich meat sauce, my father had finished the metanism and it sat in the centre of the table as we ate.

I said: "I've decided to live in the room at the Very Tall House Near The Square. I think I'll like it there. I like the Siisters."

"I thought as much," my father said. "When will you leave?"

"Tomorrow," I told him.

"Good," he said. "I hope you'll come back sometimes, though. Your mother will miss you."

"I will miss you both," I said.

"You will have larger things to think about," he said. "That's the way of it. It cannot be helped."

When we finished eating my father looked at his latest metanism for a long time in silence. It was as if he was seeing it for the first time, or remembering something from a very long time ago. Finally he reached out a hand and with a delicate finger he touched a small brass button on the top.

The metanism made a small ticking sound. From its roundness two copper wings sprang out, like the carapace of beetles. Suddenly it chattered and the wings beat and it rose in the air and described circles above our heads. In the lamplight it cast shadows like moths and it glistened and glowed like the burnished metals it was.

When it was nearly exhausted – which didn't take long – my father held out his large, dry hand and the metanism landed upon it as if it knew. It folded its wings and was still.

"I was making this and I didn't know why," he said. "But now we do."

I finished feeling the feeling of its release and nodded. "I think it may be one of your best," I said.

"I think you may be right," he said. "I think it may be one for the Library. Perhaps you would take it there for me, if it's no trouble."

"I'd be glad to," I said. "It's certainly one for the Library. I think it's one of your best."

My father nodded. He looked at the metanism on his hand for a moment longer, then curled his long dry fingers around it.

"I have enjoyed having you as my daughter," he said. "It is a simple thing – much more simple than the metanisms – but it is a good thing, too."

When he said it I knew what he meant. I knew what it meant. We didn't need to speak of it further. When I stood up from the table I went and stood behind him and put my arms around his shoulders and kissed the back of his head.

"I might not take the metanism to the Library straight away," I told him. "If that is all right. I think I might need to keep it for a little while first."

"Of course," my father said. "I know you'll do what is best."

IN THE MORNING

In the morning my father was Gone.

Before he was Gone he had laid out the breakfast things on the table and in the centre of my plate was a polished wooden box. It was a perfect cube and the wood was dark with solid brass hinges. Inside it was his last metanism.

I looked for my father in the house even though I knew he wouldn't be there. That is the way of it.

After I'd eaten breakfast I looked in on my mother and stood there for a while. After I'd done that I collected some things in a bag before I left. I took the metanism in its polished box, wrapped in a woollen sweater.

NOT THERE

Now I must describe something which I didn't see. It happened on Faer is-Land when I wasn't there. I was on my way to see my father and crossing the bridge to Fryst Is-land when it happened.

The path was dry and worn through the grass so that dust rose a little by their heels. Marianna's skirt swished against the grass on either side of the path. She walked ahead of Martin and Dot and Patrice in that order and she did so as if she was alone. Very many people are alone on the Is-lands so it is easy to imagine that you are even if you are not.

Martin carried the kitbag and Dot carried the small cardboard suitcase. Patrice walked with a hand on the canvas bag which hung against his chest. The sun was warm and the wetness started to dry from their possessions leaving salty tidemarks.

After half an hour or so they had left the shore path and risen to the top of the hill. Below them the valley was laid out in neat fields with stone walls and hedges, very well kept. It looked perfect in the sunshine and Wendell's Place was at the very end of the track they were now descending.

Wendell wasn't there. He was with the sheep and it was a long way to come back to the house. He knew of the Arrival and that Marianna would be able to take care of it even if he wasn't there, so he stayed with the sheep.

THE FIRST SIGN OF TROUBLE

Wendell's Place is a small cottage painted white. It has thick walls which make the inside cool. The windows are small and square. Outside there are barns and byres and a few carts. A single elm stands in the centre of the yard and its shadow moves like a sundial across the outbuildings.

Marianna led Martin, Dot and Patrice through the Home Meadow to the guest accommodation which had a wooden door painted yellow. When Dot saw this she spoke for the first time. She stopped and put down the small cardboard suitcase and said: "I can't stay there."

It was the first sign of trouble.

"Perhaps we can paint the door," Martin said.

"I don't think Wendell would like that," Marianna said. "I know he likes yellow."

"I think you'll get used to it," Martin told Dot.

"You might get used to it," Dot told him. "You have the patience of an Ox."

"Let's see what colour it is on the inside," he said.

Marianna led the way to the door and she worked the wooden latch so that the door opened outwards. On the other side the door was the colour of newly churned butter.

"See?" Martin said. "That's more like it. It's like the colour of the—" Then he stopped himself because he must have remembered the Rule about not speaking of what has been left.

"I'm not sure," Dot said.

"I'm sure we can live with it," Martin told her. His voice was patient and comforting.

"I'm not sure," Dot said again, but after a moment she took her husband's hand with hers. "I suppose so," she said.

"Shall we go inside?" Martin asked. He turned to look at Patrice who had still said nothing from the moment they arrived at the beach. He said nothing now.

"Lets go in," Martin said. "We need to unpack."

He led the way inside, taking Dot with him by the hand. When they were over the threshold and into the dark interior (the darkness was caused by the shutters on the windows) they vanished from sight and Patrice let out a little cry. He rushed towards the doorway, only stopping when he was close enough to see that the others had not been swallowed whole and disappeared in the interior.

He could see them standing in the centre of the room, letting their eyes adjust to the dimness and smelling the smell of a place which was dry but had not be lived in for years. He seemed relieved to see them there and he took a single step over the threshold to join them in the cool, dry-floored dimness.

"Wendell will introduce himself when he gets back from the sheep," Marianna told them. "He'll be pleased to see you're here. I'll leave you to open the shutters now."

She started off along the track and she thought that the first sign of trouble had faded and passed.

THE ROOM IN THE VERY TALL HOUSE NEAR THE SQUARE

My room was the highest in the house and it was a very tall house. There were 89 steps between the Flying Horse Tea Room in the basement and the door of my room. It did not do to go all the way down to the tea room and remember that you had left a thing that you wanted upstairs in your room.

I had put my things in a bag. I had said goodbye to my mother. I had collected the ice lizard from the track. I had left my coat in the Waiting Room. I had walked to the Very Tall House Near The Square. I had gone in the front door and carried my bag up the 77 steps from there to my room. I had done these things in that order.

From the window of my room I could see over the roofs of the town to the roundness of the rolled hills, as if I had climbed the mast of a tall ship. Sometimes the rolled hills looked like the frozen green swell of the sea and sometimes the house would creak like the rigging of a tall ship.

I put my things in the drawers and cupboards where I wanted them. I had not brought many things from Fryst is-Land. If I wanted something I hadn't brought I knew it would be just as I'd left it if I went back.

In my room there was a small table below the window which cast a patch of sunlight. That was where I placed my collection of cloud-faces and my collection of ice lizards. I was a little worried that the position would be too warm for the ice lizards but they seemed all right.

Between the lizards and the faces I placed the polished wooden box, lined with velvet, into which my father had placed his last metanism. I knew from the care he'd taken in polishing the box that he was pleased and proud of the metanism, perhaps more than any other. I would take it to the Library but I did not want to do that just yet. For a while I still wanted it with me in the room.

When I had my things arranged in the places I wanted them I went down the 89 steps to the Flying Horse Tea Room and drank tea and ate cake with the Siisters. I told them about the Arrival and about going to see my father for the last time. They gave me some flowers to take back to my room. They also gave me a vase.

"Welcome to our house," they said. It was quite formal. The Siisters were wearing long dresses that day.

THE TOWN AND THE SQUARE

The next day was Exchange & Mart Day.

Once I had collected the eggs and walked back down the long garden to the Very Tall House I told the Siisters I would be going out for a while. They understood. I left them in the Tea Room and went to the Square in Town. The Square is near to the Very Tall House. It is a one minute walk.

I should tell about the Town and the Square now.

We only called it the Town because it had to be called something. It wasn't so large, but larger than Fryst Village which was the only other place in the is-lands with more than three houses together.

The Square in the centre of Town had broad-leaved horse chestnut trees at each corner. These provided shade and were very pleasant.

At the centre of the Square there was a well which wasn't a well but an iron pipe which spouted water from a mossy stone into a rusted grate below. The well was often where people met and spoke even when it wasn't Exchange & Mart Day. Speaking to people in Town was one of the reasons for living there. There were plenty of places in the is-lands where you did not have to speak to anyone but yourself, and not even to yourself if you didn't want to, but there was only one Town.

(In Fryst Village people will talk to each other also, but it is usually too cold to stand in the street to do that. Also, the days are very short and if people have things to do while it is light they do not want to spend daylight in talking. If you want to speak to someone in Fryst Village you generally go to their house or they come to yours once it is dark.)

INTERCOURSE

Because it was Exchange & Mart Day in Town there were numerous people stopping and speaking to each other in the Square and at the Hall.

The Hall was to the left of the Square. There were many buildings in the is-lands which were unlike any other and the Hall was one of them. It was a dark building made of dark red bricks which had a sheen like varnish. Its walls were not even as tall as I am and the roof was flat and covered with thick lead. It might be that the weight of all that lead had slowly pushed the Hall down into the ground. It felt as if that might be the case. You entered the hall by going down steps which never saw the sun. It was another place where people would go to meet together or to see Charlie, Mr Meyer.

Around the Hall people had set out their wares on the flat roof. There were snap-apples and paintings; jams and scissors; cakes and hooch. Some people just sat on the edge of the roof, dangling their legs off it, waiting to see who would be interested in them.

Some people made more of an effort than others. Some had dressed neatly and brought their exchange items in smart baskets lined with linen. Some had brought handcarts which were painted in bright colours and sometimes had names like *Susan* or *Sunrise*. These marters always attracted people who wanted exchange and they would do trade along with intercourse about each other's lives and doings. Sometimes it was just enough to exchange a story for a pound of plums if all one person wanted was a story and the other liked the look of the plums.

To get where I was going I had to cross the Square and pass the Hall. I spoke to several people as I did that. I told a different thing to each person, but only one thing because I was not really in the mood for long talks. Some people didn't realise this and wanted me to tell more. Several asked about the Arrival the day before but if I'd already told them something else I didn't tell them any more about it. I would say "Ask Bill or Linda." I'd already told them.

I told Christine flower that my father had Gone. She knew I didn't want to say more than that. That was why I told her. She gave me a knotted string of stones in exchange for the telling.

A few steps later I met Marianna who didn't ask me anything but she told me how it had been when she took Martin and Dot and Patrice to Wendell's Place. She told me about the yellow door.

"I thought it might be the first sign of trouble," she told me. "But I think it was all right in the end. I'm pretty sure."

Even though I didn't speak to anyone for long it was already half morning before I had crossed the square and passed the Hall and left all the intercourse behind me.

Ω

The other place I should tell about here is the Harbour. It is the end of the Town, or the beginning. It is where I went after I had left the Square.

If you were to rise up in a balloon and look down you would see that the Harbour is a Ω shape. The entrance between the quay walls is as narrow as two footpaths side by side. It is just enough for a boat, which is all it needs to be.

The boats here were all long and slim – perhaps a dozen. Their curled dragon prows nuzzled up to the harbour wall like piglets to the sow, or rested askew, half up on the sand beach. These boats all knew their way home, which was a good thing when their swains had opened a bottle or two as they waited for their nets or their pots to come full.

Those who fished as their Work were a stand-offish bunch. Men like French and Simian fisher (of whom I'll tell later) and Bill nails and trout Field (who only appear here). After a day's Works they would sit on the harbour and chew fat in the sun, and when it was dark – and sometimes when not – they would repair to the Harbourside In and drink apple cider. They were happy with their own company, by and large, and did not mix much beyond it. They liked the company of those who would also see the beauty in the globe of a fish eye and the barnacled back of a lobster or crab.

I WAIT FOR SOME TIME

There is a very pretty beach of white sand in the curve of the harbour and behind that is a wall and a coarse grassy place. On that grassy place is the Waiting Bench. It is one of the oldest artefacts in the is-lands. It may be *the* oldest, there is no way to tell now. It is a single, thick plank nailed at each end to a log. The nails have square heads and there are eight altogether. The bench smells sweet and new-cut. It hasn't weathered a day since it was put there. The nails haven't rusted.

The bench is just the right height for sitting on. There is nothing to lean back against but it is long enough to lie down on if you don't mind your feet hanging over one end. Pink-tinged daisies grow in the grass beneath it.

This was where I sat when I came to the harbour.

I wasn't waiting *for* anything. That didn't matter. I was just waiting.

No-one will bother you if they see you on the Waiting Bench, unless, that is, you are waiting for them. And if you are waiting for them then they aren't bothering you when they approach because they are what you were waiting for.

When you sit and just wait on the bench you always know when you should keep on waiting and when you have waited enough. That is what the feeling of the waiting bench is. That is why it was made.

Whoever made it knew what they were doing. They fed that bench with waiting. It may have taken many years to do that. They may have made and rejected any number of other benches – some with backs, some longer or shorter or more fancy. In the end, though, they made the waiting bench just right and it is still there, waiting, although the person who made it is Gone.

I waited for some time on the bench. No-one bothered me. I sat and lay and sat again on the bench. When I had waited enough it was dark.

NIGHT IN TOWN

When I walked back to the Very Tall House Near The Square I heard cider-songs from the Harbourside In. This wasn't unusual after an Exchange & Mart Day. The windows were lit against the dark.

As I passed through the Square I saw a small group of people standing beside the steps which led down to the entrance to the Hall. These people stood together without a light. There was a faint light from the door to the Hall so I knew it stood open below. I thought perhaps the group of people were about to go into the Hall, or maybe they had just come out from it to talk privately.

I did not know what part of the night it was, but I thought it must be pretty late. That was how it felt. I wondered why these people were standing outside the Hall so I looked at them as I went past. They were talking quietly and privately. I could tell that one of the people was Charlie, Mr Meyer. Only he had blond curls like that, which I saw in the faint light even though he had his back to me.

The other person I knew who they were was Martin. I saw a reflection on his large, round spectacles. That was how I knew. The others were gathered around him and I could tell he was saying something serious in a low voice. I was pretty sure that Dot and Patrice were not with him and I thought that was unusual.

For a moment I thought it was unusual enough that I ought to go across to them and enquire. Then I thought that I didn't feel like being involved, whatever it was, so I just said "Good evening, One and All" very politely as I passed.

Martin stopped talking then and after a moment I heard Charlie say, "Good evening, Issy."

Nothing more was said as I crossed the Square. It was very quiet there, and on the road to the Very Tall House.

I let myself in at the front door and heard the sound of the sewing machine from behind the Siisters' door. I counted the stairs as I went up so that I would know when I had reached my room.

INVITATIONS TO A TEA DANCE

I think the Siisters could tell I was still feeling sad because my father had Gone. One morning Simone said to me: "We are going to have a Tea Dance. We would like you to take the invitations to the people we would like to be there."

"Will you do that?" Elaine asked. "It may take a couple of days."

"Of course," I said. I liked helping the Siisters in the Tea Rooms but it would be pleasant to go out for a while.

Elaine handed me a small bundle of parchment letters, each inscribed with a name in broad, soot-black ink. The bundle was tied with a piece of raffia in a bow. There were thirteen letters so I knew it would not be a large tea dance.

When the Siisters went to the kitchen to beat eggs I sat at the table nearest the window and opened the bundle of letters to see who they were destined for. I had to know this in order to deliver them. The names were:

Per si-Lversum

Sam Hall

Charlie, Mr Meyer

Wendell (Martin & Dot & Patrice)

Nancé the Teacher

Issy

There were seven other names but they don't matter here.

My own letter was at the bottom of the pile. I opened it, folding the parchment back like the opening of a flower so that I could read the writing inside. It said "*Dear Issy, we would like to invite you to a Tea Dance ten days from now. To be held at the Flying Horse Tea Room. You know where that is. Mid-afternoon. With love from Elaine and Simone.*"

THE FIRST DELIVERY

Just then I heard the gate snick as it tried to bite the hand that had freed it. It didn't succeed, though. I looked up and saw feet coming down the granite steps and knew it was Charlie, Mr Meyer. Charlie was too smart for that gate.

When he came into the Tea Room the bell on the door tinkled and when he looked round I smiled. "Hello, Charlie," I said.

"Hello Issy," he said. "I hoped you were here. I hoped I might get tea and an egg on toast. Poached."

"Poached are the best," I told him.

He came and sat down in the chair across the table from me. He folded his hands very neatly on the tablecloth in front of him. He looked at the pile of letters. "Have you been writing?" he asked.

I told him I hadn't. I said that Simone and Elaine had written the letters and that they were invitations to a Tea Dance which I was going to deliver. I took his letter from the bundle and handed it to him. "You're my first delivery," I said.

"Thank you," he said. He didn't open the letter but slipped it into his pocket, making sure the flap on the pocket was closed over it so that it wouldn't be lost by accident.

"So you've moved here," he said.

I told him I had. I told him how many steps there were to my room. He nodded.

"I also have an invitation," he said then. "You are invited to the Hall. We would like to talk to you about something."

"I had imagined you would," I said. "When would you like me to come to talk about it?"

"Perhaps the day after the tea dance would be best," he said. "That will give you time to deliver these invitations and not worry about having to come to the Hall. Would that be all right?"

"Of course. It will be easy to remember."

"Good."

"Shall I ask the Siisters to poach your egg now?"

"Thank you."

A PLAN

It is impossible to draw maps of the is-lands. Even if you try you will not get it right. When you look again you will realise that this hill or this cove is in the wrong place. Trying to draw a map is like mixing water and oil in a bottle. It can be pretty but it is of no use as a map.

While Charlie, the Meyer, ate his poached egg I sat at another table and spread the invitations on the table cloth in front of me. I had decided to deliver them according to where I would find the invitees. Even without a map I knew where I should go.

I put all the invitations for people who lived in Town together. I would deliver these first, I thought.

Then I put together all the invitations to people who lived on Faer but not in Town. These included Wendell (Martin & Dot & Patrice) and three others whose names don't matter here.

That left just one which was for Sam Hall who lived on Hallows is-Land. I would take that one last because it was the farthest away.

I tied each different bundle of invitations together with string from behind the counter and told the Siisters of my plan while they watched Charlie eat his egg. They agreed it was a good plan. They were keen that I started to make deliveries as soon as possible. They were already looking forward to the Tea Dance.

MORE DELIVERIES

Elaine lent me her bicycle to make the deliveries. This made things easier.

I carried the bundles of letters in the basket attached to the handlebars. The name of the next recipient was upwards so that I could see who they were and where I should be peddling to. By the afternoon end I had delivered all the invitations to the nine invitees who lived in Town.

You might think that it took me a long time just to deliver nine invitations and you would be right. It was a time-consuming task.

When I first arrived the invitees would be in their house or their garden or sitting in the shade of a jasmine bush. They would say something like "Hello, Issy. What brings you here on a bicycle?"

Then I would say something like: "The Siisters asked me to bring you a letter." Then I would hand it to them.

I wouldn't tell them what the letter was about because I didn't want to spoil the surprise, so the person would be puzzled at first. They would look at the thick black ink with which their name was written and then, when they were sure that the letter was really for them, they would open it.

That was the part I liked watching the most. They would open the letter and read it. Sometimes they would read it again. Then they would be surprised by what they had read: that they were invited to a Tea Dance. They were surprised because no such thing had been done before at the Flying Horse Tea Room, or anywhere else. Sometimes they would say that.

PER

Per si-Lversum looked up from his letter and said: "I've never heard of such a thing. It's most unusual. Most."

"Three people have said that," I told him. "May I tell the Siisters you will come?"

"You may," he said. "Although I'm not certain it's a good idea."

Per was burning a small camp fire just outside his hut. A coffee pot was hanging over the embers keeping warm. After looking at the letter for a second time he fed it to the camp fire which devoured it greedily.

"Why did you say you weren't certain it was a good idea, Per?" I asked him. Like Christine flowers, Per si-Lversum was a person who would give you a straight answer if that was what you wanted.

"You have to ask yourself *why now*?" he said. "Those Siisters, much as I like them, they never do anything for no reason."

He reached to take the coffee off the fire but forgot that it would be hot. When he touched the handle he let go again quickly, then sucked his fingers.

"I have a bad feeling," he said. "I think it may be the first sign of trouble."

"I think it must be the second sign of trouble," I corrected him.

I told him about what Marianna had told me about Dot not liking the colour of the guest house door at Wendell's Place and how Marianna had thought it was the first sign of trouble for a while.

"That's an interesting story," Per said when I had finished telling it. "Would you like a cup of joe? This time I'll remember to use a cloth to pick up the pot."

NANCÉ

When Nancé the Teacher read her letter she was quiet for a long time afterwards. I didn't think anything of it at the time. I thought it was because she was thinking about what an unusual thing a Tea Dance would be. I thought she might be considering what one would wear on such an occasion. Nancé was always well turned out.

Today she was wearing a long and short gown of yellow muslin in several layers. The innermost layers were short and the outermost layers were long. When she moved through the yellow patch of sunlight coming in through the window the gown disappeared as if she was wearing nothing at all.

In the end Nancé said: "Will you thank the Siisters for their kind invitation?"

I said that I would, but the way that she'd said it made me think that she would not be coming to the Tea Dance. If so she would be the first person to decline.

"Will you come?" I asked then, because she still hadn't said yes or no. "You can RSVI if you like (which means Reply Soon Via Issy)."

"I'm afraid—" Nancé said. But the way that she said it made it sound like half a sentence written up on the blackboard. I waited to see what she would say/write next.

"—I am quite busy. I've just finished another embroidery but now I've seen that it's flawed."

She fingered the outer layer of her muslin gown.

"I'm sure that's not true," I said. I was being polite.

"No, no, it is," Nancé said. "Somehow there always seems to be one stitch that is wrong. I don't know how I don't spot it, but I never do. Not until later, and by then it's too late. Just one stitch in the wrong place is enough. See here."

She lifted a delicate embroidery of purple and green, still in its frame, from where it rested in the sunlight of the tall window. As she stood in the sunlight her gown disappeared. When she brought the embroidery to me the gown returned.

I put down my porcelain tea cup and took the embroidery in its frame. It had a design which looked like house martins, swooping. I looked at it carefully but I couldn't see a wrong stitch even though I looked for a long time.

"You would find it in the end," Nancé told me. "And then you would see it every time you looked at the thing. Your eye would be drawn to it and you'd be unable to look at anything else.

That's the way of it. It may not get you at first, but in the end it always will."

As I ran my hand over the cloth I could sense its deep feeling of longing and then my finger found the wrong stitch like the sharp prick of a needle.

"Ouch," I said, feeling its loss and the tiny, sharp prick of regret. There might have been ten thousand stitches but it was that *one* which would still have the power to prick you every time you ran a hand across the cloth, no matter how many other stitches there were.

Nancé nodded sadly. "You see what I mean," she said.

"Yes, I see."

A tiny ball of red blood had formed on my finger. I sucked it and slowly the regret subsided.

"Sometimes I think there may be no end," Nancé said. She handled the embroidery carefully by the frame as I handed it back to her. "Then I wonder what I shall do."

"Perhaps a Tea Dance is just what you need," I said, not wishing to make things worse.

"Perhaps it is," she said, and the idea seemed to lift her spirits. "I shall make a new dress," Nancé told me. "I think I have time if I start today. I'm sure of it."

"I had better leave you to start, then," I told her.

Nancé was my last delivery in Town. I was pleased with my progress. When I returned to the Tea Room I told the Siisters that everyone who had received an invitation so far would be coming to the Tea Dance. They were pleased about that, too.

EXPERIMENTS

I was keen to continue with the delivering of letters. When I awoke the next day I went straight down to the kitchen. I had already smelled the aroma of cooking. It had risen 77 steps from the kitchen all the way to my room. The Siisters had clearly been cooking for some time even though it was early.

I said good morning to the Siisters when I entered the kitchen. They shooed me out again as quickly as they could, with flaps from their aprons and the waving of spoons. I sensed that they were making experiments and did not wish to be observed.

I was not allowed to have breakfast in the kitchen as I normally did. Instead the Siisters served me poached eggs in the Flying Horse Tea Room, as if I was a paying customer (although they did not give me a bill).

Afterwards I stood up from the table and told the Siisters I would be delivering the remaining invitations today. They were pleased about that. Elaine wrapped some food in a cloth and tied it with string. She said it was provisions for the journey. I think she was feeling guilty for waving her spoon and nearly flicking me with gravy.

GOING TO WENDELL'S PLACE

By the time it was nearly midday I had delivered three more invitations which only left Wendell and Sam Hall to visit.

It was a good Faer day and Elaine's bicycle hummed as I rode the lanes. I was glad I was riding it. I liked the feeling of the wind against by body. I also liked riding through those places where the trees overhung the lanes and made dapples of shade and sunlight. If you ride fast enough through them the whole world seems to flicker.

I stopped twice to collect cloud-faces but only one was good enough to keep. It looked like someone's father last thing at night.

WENDELL'S PLACE

If you look down on Wendell's Place from the top of Borrow Hill (which is the way to get to it if you are riding a bicycle along the lanes) then you can see that the fields are all square. Each has a stone wall around it. Each field has two gates – one into it, one out of it. Some of the fields will be a rich brown of turned dirt; some will be a honey yellow of ripe wheat; some will be the dark green of un-grazed grass and some will be a lighter green, dotted with the whiteness of sheep. Sometimes you will see the red shirt that Wendell is wearing.

The track to Wendell's Place was bumpy and winding. The bumps made my teeth chatter as I rode the bicycle down it. *Brrrrrrrr.*

I was thinking about Martin and Dot and Patrice as I reached the gate to the yard and dismounted. I was wondering how they had settled in after their Arrival.

As I wheeled the bicycle into the yard I saw that the Guest House door was blue. I thought maybe Marianna had told me the wrong colour when she had said it was yellow, but as I got closer I saw that the paint on the door was new and it hadn't been applied very well. In places it had run and in others you could still see small patches of yellow beneath. It looked as if someone had done it in a hurry.

The door was closed and I didn't knock. I thought that I should find Wendell because his name was first on the front of the letter. I hadn't seen his red shirt in the fields so I thought he was probably somewhere close by his place, unless he had taken a flock beyond the River and the Woods, which he sometimes did. His flocks will follow him anywhere.

I wheeled the bicycle into the yard in front of Wendell's cottage and that was where I saw him. He was in the very centre of the yard. He was standing with Martin and Dot and Charlie, Mr Meyer. It took me a moment to see Patrice. He was sitting on an up-turned bucket near the barn.

Seeing Charlie there was a surprise to me. I think that seeing me walk into the yard was a surprise to Charlie, too. He looked for a moment as if it was not a thing he had expected to happen but then – because he has to be polite as the Meyer – he smiled and raised a hand in greeting.

When he did this all the others except Patrice turned to look at me as well. They had been standing together as if they were at each corner of a square. I knew from the way they were standing that they had been discussing something important and not just passing the time of day. Because of the way they stood I was reminded of seeing Charlie and Martin in the square at night even though it was a bright daylight now.

"Good morning, One and All," I said.

"Good morning, Issy," Charlie said. "What brings you out here today?"

He said it like someone who is not convinced you will give them a straight answer.

"I'm making deliveries for the Siisters," I told him straight.

"Ah, yes," he said with a nod. "I understand now."

I lay the bicycle down carefully on the ground and took the next to last letter over to Wendell.

Wendell was a round man who had to consider his actions carefully before he made them. If he made an action too quickly he would go red in the face to match his shirt.

"Thank you, Issy," he said as he considered the letter. Then he took it.

"You're welcome," I told him. "I see you've painted the door of the Guest House."

A REQUEST

No-one spoke for several moments. Wendell held the letter but did not open it. Martin looked at Dot and then at Charlie, Mr Meyer. It was as if they were speaking without sound or moving their mouths. I thought this so strongly that I opened my mouth wide to make my ear drums pop. It made no difference.

"I would like to make a request of you, Issy," Charlie said then.

"I'm not sure I have time for requests," I said. "I still have one more invitation to deliver. It's for Sam Hall."

"Of course," he said. "That must come first."

I was curious though. I said: "Perhaps if you told me the request I might be able to help – if it doesn't interfere with the delivery. Perhaps one would not exclude the other."

"Perhaps not," Charlie said. He looked at the others. Martin nodded.

"We would like to ask you to talk to Patrice," Charlie told me. "Perhaps he could accompany you part of the way on your delivery. We feel it would be... good: good if he was to talk to someone other than ourselves for a while."

"Does he want to talk?" I asked them. I looked at Patrice who did not seem like he craved conversation. He looked as much like talking as a stone.

"I think he will in the end," Charlie said. "He hasn't spoken since the Arrival."

"Do you think he's ill?" I asked.

"We don't think so," Martin said. "We think he just needs the right opportunity."

"What would you like me to talk to him about?" I asked Charlie.

"Anything you like," he said. "We'll leave that to you. There are a lot of things you could tell him about. Perhaps something will take his interest."

"I think I can do that without interfering with the delivery," I said.

"Thank you," Dot said. It was the first time she had spoken. "We appreciate it."

"I'll tell him," Martin said.

LEAVING WENDELL'S PLACE

Before we left I asked Wendell if I could have a piece of paper and a pencil. He said I could and fetched them from his house. I sat down on a log and wrote a list of subjects that I thought might interest Patrice. I wrote down six:

The Town
The Errid Shelter
The Süsters
My Father
The Library
Whelme

Wendell said I should keep the pencil in case I thought of more things or wanted to write something else.

When I was ready to go I picked up the bicycle and wheeled it towards the gate where Patrice and Martin were standing. As I approached I heard Martin say: "We trust you."

Martin opened the gate and I went through. Martin patted Patrice on the shoulder and he followed me. No-one said anything else.

TO SPEAK OR NOT TO SPEAK

"I have made a list of things that I could tell you about if you would like me to talk about them," I said to Patrice.

I handed him the list.

"Or I can talk about something else," I said. "But you will have to tell me what would interest you because I can't guess."

As we walked the bicycle made a click-click-click to accompany us. I wasn't riding it, of course.

"Or we can not speak," I said.

We were following a sheep path towards the River because that was the way to go to Hallows from Wendell's Place. The sheep walked away from us on their stiff, sheep-stilt legs. They spilled neat little dung balls the size of sloeberries as they went.

"I am a prodigy," Patrice said then. "That is why we are here. Martin and Dot only brought me because they had to. I would rather have stayed. I lived in a palace. Now I am supposed to live in a shack with a yellow/blue door."

"You mustn't speak of before," I told him. "Didn't you hear the Rule?"

"I'm tired of Rules," Patrice said. "Where we came from had Rules. There were Rules about everything: who you can talk to, what you must do, what you must *not* do and with whom. Why is this place any different if you're going to keep telling me about the Rule? I thought we were coming to a place *without* Rules. I thought that was why we came."

"There is only one Rule here," I told him. "And it's for the best."

"So *you* say," he said. "But if you don't speak of that Somewhere – if you won't let *us* speak of it – how do you know that you even *need* your stupid Rule any more. How do you know? Maybe you *don't* need it any more."

"We must do," I said. "Otherwise you wouldn't be here."

When I said that Patrice scowled at me. It was the sort of scowl a person makes when they know that you are right but they don't want to admit it.

"It's for the best," I said and I tried to make my voice sound gentle and comforting.

When I said it he put a hand over the bag next to his chest as if to protect it. He wouldn't speak again for some time so we walked in silence.

THE LIST

"Tell me about The Town," Patrice said. He had been reading the list. He had read it several times.

"It isn't for everyone," I said. "But those who live there like it. It is sociable."

"Tell me about the Errid Shelter."

"It is fascinating," I said. "Not many people know of it. I might be the only one. It smells of deep, deep earth."

"The Siisters."

"Elaine and Simone. This is Elaine's bicycle. They run the Flying Horse Tea Room. You will meet them soon enough if you come to the Tea Dance which was the invitation I brought. You are included."

"Your father."

"He's Gone now. I don't wish to talk about that. I have changed my mind."

"The Library."

I smiled at that. "Without the Library we would be nothing," I said. "It is the reason for the is-lands. It is why we are here. The Library is Hope. There are cots in some of its rooms for those who wish to spend more time within it. Sometimes it is busy, sometimes it isn't. Whatever you want to know about the Library and how it works and what is contained there you can find out from aüggie. He would like to tell you, I'm sure. I will introduce you."

"Whelme," Patrice said.

"That is where I was born," I said. "I am the first and only person to be born in the is-lands. I was born as my parents made their Arrival on the beach. I was told about it. I wasn't there until my mother put her feet on the sand and then I made my Arrival. That is what I was told. A short while later my mother was Gone but my father and I continued to live on Whelme for some time after that."

He thought about what I had said. It was the only thing he had thought about from the things I'd told him about.

"So why are you here?" he asked when he was ready.

"I just told you," I said. "Because I was born here."

"That can't be right," he said. "You can't be here if you don't know why you're here. That isn't how it goes."

"I think I should know how it goes since I've been here all my life and you have only been here a few days," I said. I didn't regret the tone of my voice.

THE NUMBERS

A while later we reached the River. It was cool there and nicely edged by the regular stone blocks. The River in this place was six inches deep and as wide as two people head to toe. It was as clear as an eye and the gravel at the bottom was predominantly yellow and shades thereof. It made you want to take off your shoes and stand in it so I did.

I laid Elaine's bicycle in the grass. While I took off my shoes and stockings Patrice stood away from the edge of the River but he watched me. He didn't say anything as I stepped down off the edging stones and into the water, feeling the semi-sharp roundness of the gravel on my soles.

I could tell that Patrice wanted to take off his shoes and socks and stand in the River. He looked at the water hungrily but he didn't come to the edge. Instead he sat down on a stone surrounded by long grass. He seemed to resent the fact that he didn't come and stand in the River.

"I know the number of things," he said to me then. "I know the number of fish in the sea. I know the blades of grass and the sand on Silvermine beach. But I can't tell you these numbers. They are too large and by the time I'd told you the number it would be wrong. If a number isn't true I can't say it."

I thought about this as a trout brushed my ankle.

"Tell me a number that *was* true then," I said.

"What number?"

I looked to my left where the meadow swept upwards in a broad brush stroke under a silent, lone elm, reaching.

"The leaves on the elm," I said. "When I say 'now' tell me the number that was true for that moment of the 'now'."

"Are you sure?" he asked.

"Yes," I said. "Now."

He looked at the lone elm. There was no wind to shake the branches and no falling of leaves.

"One," he said. "There might as well be one. Compared to the fish and the sand and the grass in the world that tree is one. Perhaps less than one."

I thought about that as the trout swam away. I didn't say anything.

Patrice looked at me then. "I know your numbers," he said. "They aren't so large."

I looked down at my feet through the soft water.

"Shall I tell you?"

I shook my head. "No. Thank you."

"Three and seven and ten and zero."

I continued to look at my feet, watching my toes move. I thought about the numbers.

"Well?" he said.

"I'd like you to go now," I said. "I asked you not to say, but you did. That wasn't very nice."

"Numbers can't be nice or not nice," he said. "They are just numbers. It's what they count that you like or don't like. But it's not the fault of the numbers."

"How do you know?" I said. "How do you know what the numbers are."

"I see them," he said. "When I see you I see your numbers. They are what you are. You are the sum of the numbers."

"I'd like you to go now," I said once again.

"That's what they all say."

"That's what a person *will* say when they ask you not to tell them numbers and you tell them anyway."

"I only tell true numbers," he said.

"That makes no difference. Go away please."

For a moment longer he sat on the rock, then he stood up. He placed a hand on the bag against his chest and turned away. He followed the path of our footsteps to get there. I wiggled my toes in the water. I didn't like Patrice and what he had told me.

HALLOWS

I left Elaine's bicycle under a tree before I walked to the bridge. I didn't want it to rust and for the honey smooth-running oil in the gears to become black and choked and for the tyres to perish and go flat. I didn't think Elaine would like to get it back like that. I was being responsible.

The Hallows bridge is of golden hamstone and it arches high across the divide which is only thirty three paces wide. It is a beautiful bridge with a roundness that looks like a pregnant woman lying on her back, cut in stone, full and happy.

Once I had crossed over I passed three people returning to the bridge with baskets over their arms. They had apples and mushrooms and plums and pears in the baskets and they all walked swiftly to cross the bridge before these things could rot.

There are lots of paths through the woods and the open fields of Hallows is-Land. There is no single track that one should take to get anywhere. The paths are all narrow and criss-cross each other. They are like a length of dropped cord. You follow one till it crosses another and then you take the other and so on until you get where you're going.

As I took the path to the left away from the bridge and into the woods the mist still hung damp and shroud-still between the leaves of the trees. The leaves were tinged orange and yellow at their tips, the way they always are in the morning. Spider webs laced the redding clusters of apples and shone silver.

When I emerged on a second path I was higher up the hill. The sunlight was golden and the apples were falling with dull thuds whether you listened or not.

SAM HALL

I reached Sam Hall's house where it sat on the hillside above the trees and looked out on the mist and the sunlight over it.

The house was made of grey planks and red roof tiles greened with moss. I knew that inside there were only two rooms. It was a simple house, wrapped round with a porch of steel plates riveted together. The steel plates were a dark, tanned brown as if they had been in the sea for a long time.

When I arrived at the house Sam Hall was tending the garden. He had a hoe and a bucket and he was tilling the black earth between lettuce and peas, squashes and tomatoes. It was very neat. Surgical, even.

"Hello, Sam," I said.

"Hello, Issy," he said and his voice was smiling so I knew he was glad to see me. "What brings you to see me?"

"My feet," I said. It was a joke we shared.

"Boy, I'm pleased to see you," he said.

Sam Hall wore boots that were grey with dried earth and had leather laces. At the other end he had long dark hair and a beard. In between he wore dungarees.

I remembered the delicious things that Elaine and Simone had wrapped up for me. I was hungry by now and I thought it would be good to share the things with Sam if we sat on the steps to the porch.

We were just in time. We ate several cakes but the ones we did not eat in time turned stale while they waited. The egg and tomato sandwiches were still fine, though. We ate all of them.

When we'd finished eating I took the last invitation from my pocket and gave it to Sam. He brushed crumbs from his beard and unfolded the paper after reading his name on the front. He looked at the invitation and made a small sound with his lips as he read.

NEEDS

"Those Siisters have needs," he said after he'd read. "Is that why they've invited me?"

"I wouldn't know," I said. "What sort of needs do you mean?"

"It varies," he said. "Or it has in the past. I'm not so sure I shall go. Sometimes it's too much. Sometimes just the thought of it is too much. The garden will rot if I go."

"I'm sure they would understand that," I said. "Whatever their needs are. They understand gardens."

"They do that," Sam said, nodding.

I looked out over the garden. At the centre of the onion patch there was a sturdy tripod of wood and iron and on top of it was mounted a shiny dish the size of a walnut. In front of the dish was a glass lens on a rack and pinion gear.

"Is that a new one?" I asked.

Sam nodded. "It is A HISTORY OF THE IS-LANDS," he said. "I think it will be a good evening to try it again. But I don't have it right yet. It may take a while."

"I hope it does," I said. "I would like you to be here a while yet."

Sam was quiet for a while then. When he spoke his voice was a sort of sad.

"Would you like to do the rubbing of the bodies with me again?" he asked.

"I don't know," I said. "I'm not sure it will help."

"It might help one of us," he said. "But I can see why you wouldn't be sure. That's okay."

I sat and thought about it for a time. Thinking about it helped. I could imagine that on the brass bed, on the bright squares of the patchwork quilt with the yellow sun at the window, it might be a very pleasant thing to do. I thought it would be pleasant to be naked and to watch Sam get naked to his bare bony body like a stick with the hairs on his chest.

After a while of thinking about this I stood up from the step and left my shoes there so I trod bare foot on the steps. I held out my hand.

"I think I *would* like to do the rubbing of the bodies thing with you," I told him. "I think it will help both of us."

"Thank you," he said and he took my hand.

AFTERWARDS

Afterwards Sam Hall and I lay still and warm. It had been very nice and I had been right when I thought it would help both of us.

After a while of stillness and warmth Sam Hall got off the bright squares of the quilt and put on his dungarees. I watched him and that was very nice, too.

"Would you like to stay?" he asked me. "I'm a quiet man and I think you're quiet too. That's good in a place like this."

"At the moment I can't stay," I told him. "I also have an invitation to the Tea Dance and the day after that I told Charlie, Mr Meyer that I would go to the Hall to talk with him."

"Ah," Sam said. "That's something, of course."

He sat on the edge of the bed to put on his boots.

"Perhaps you'd consider coming back instead, then," he said. "That wouldn't be exactly the same as not leaving at all."

"You're right," I said. "And I can see that this might be the place for me. I also like the rubbing of the bodies thing with you – perhaps more than—"

But as I said it Sam held up a hand. "Please don't tell me," he said. "When you live alone and there is an Issy who comes to visit once in a while it's better if those visits are islands which do not connect to any other lands. That's the way I feel about it."

"Of course, Sam," I told him and I smiled to show that I did understand.

"You're a great gal," he said then as his eyes sparkled with water. "Just great."

"What are you going to do now?" I asked.

He put his boots on the grey floorboards. "I need to tend the garden," he said.

"May I help?" I asked. "I have no more invitations to deliver. I'd like to get the dirt in my fingers and an ache in my back. Afterwards I'd like to sit on the stoop for a while and wait for evening when you can show me your HISTORY OF THE IS-LANDS even if it isn't quite right yet. Then we can eat the salad from the garden and drink sloeberry hooch – just a little – and come back to this bed and do rubbing of the bodies very slowly and longly. Then in the morning I will leave."

"You want to do *all* that?" he asked.

"All that," I said. "I feel much better. Thank you."

"Well we'd better get to it, then," he said with a chuckle, so I knew he was pleased. "All of that. My, my."

IN THE MORNING AGAIN

In the morning I felt the ache in my back like I'd wanted. I had washed the dirt from my fingers the previous evening after Sam and I had finished in the garden but there was still some of it there in the small lines and cracks. It was good to see it and remember.

I remembered that THE HISTORY OF THE ISLANDS hadn't been *quite* right yet, but even so it had been a pleasant thing to see Sam Hall turning knurled knobs and making delicate adjustments to the lenses and tripod. He hummed quietly while he did that. He was going to get it *just* right some day.

When we'd had breakfast I said goodbye to Sam, although I could tell he didn't want me to. So I changed my mind and stayed with him all day, which he did want me to.

We pulled carrots and lettuce and hoed the ground. In the evening Sam cooked a wind-fall apple stew, just in time, then I left him in peace for a while so that he could hum to himself over A HISTORY OF THE IS-LANDS as the sun set. After that we each had two glasses of sloe-berry hooch and after night it was the morning again and this time when I said goodbye to Sam Hall we both knew I meant it.

"Don't worry, Sam," I told him. "I like visiting you on Hallows is-Land. I promise I will again, soon."

"Very soon?" he asked me. "Only don't say that if you don't mean it. That's all I ask."

"Very soon," I told him.

"Good," he said. "That's all right then." And he looked happier.

I closed the gate as I left. It had a lovely latch.

ON THE WAY HOME

On the way home I remembered my father in the tick-tick-tick of the wheels of Elaine's bicycle as I walked. I remembered that I had promised to take his last metanism to the Library.

I did not have the metanism with me. It was still in my room at the top of the Very Tall House Near The Square where it sat in the sun on the table between the ice lizards and cloud-faces. But as the path I was taking would take me close to a way which led to the Library I decided to go there and tell aüggie that I would be bringing a metanism along in due course. I thought he might appreciate the notice.

When the path I was on came to a hollowed out bowl of a place with bushes and saplings over-growing it, I stopped. I leaned Elaine's bike against a post and followed my track to the red brick and stone wall with a doorway at the side. That was where I went in to the cool interior and knelt down to find the lantern I'd left there.

This is the Back Way to the Library. It was not a way that I had heard of anyone else knowing or using. It was a way I had found when I was younger and my father had been building the big lathe in the shed because he still thought he wanted to make larger things. I found the place and explored it in detail many times over although I didn't know what it was called or what it was for.

When I returned home and my father came in from the big lathe in the shed I asked him about the place I had found. That was when he told me the story about Errid.

THE ERRID STORY

Once a once a time (my father told me) *people believed that there was an evil and malevolent thing called an Errid which would take to the skies in search of the people it hated. It had their number, it knew what they were up to.*

The people had their numbers, too. They thought they would give them security, but the numbers did not. When Errid came in the sky it looked down and took away the people it counted. They were not seen again.

No-one really knew (my father went on) *when the Errid would come or who it would take next. So the people built and dug places to hide so that the Errid wouldn't see them. These places were Errid Shelters* (which was what I had found).

AFTER THE STORY

The story about the Errid frightened me somewhat. My father could see that and his face was concerned. He asked me if I would take him to see the place I had found.

The next day I took him and I could tell he felt happier when he saw that the Errid Shelter was overgrown and abandoned.

"That is because," he told me, "there is no longer an Errid. Even if an Errid existed at all it was a long time and a long way away from the is-lands. I doubt that Errid would ever have come to the is-lands, even if it had existed. The is-lands are too small and insignificant to trouble anyone, even an Errid."

I felt better when he told me that. I could see he was right.

Inside the shelter I showed my father something which had puzzled me. On pegs in the flaking whitewashed wall were five faces with large glass eyes and trunks like an elephant but ending in metal boxes.

"What are those?" I asked.

"Ah," my father said. "Those are guess masks."

He took one down from its peg in the wall and put his face in its face. I no longer knew who he was.

"They are called guess masks because when people wore them you could not tell who they were, only guess," my father said. His voice was muffled and did not sound like his voice. "If you wore one of these when the Errid passed across the sky it couldn't tell who was who and so it would pass by or return home, disappointed that it hadn't found the ones whom it sought."

When he removed the guess mask I could see that it was him again. He replaced the guess mask carefully on its peg.

I offered to show my father what else I had found in the Errid Shelter but he said that he had seen enough. He didn't want to go further into the shelter as I had done. He thought he would like to return to Fryst and continue with the larger things on the big lathe in the shed. It was later that day when he realised that larger things were not what he was seeking. From then on we used the shed just to store wood

I thought about this as I passed the guess masks and followed the passages down deep in the earth. I wondered how my father had come to realise that larger things were not for him.

I passed the rooms with rusting cots and large maps not of here. Other rooms had tables and chairs, and yet more had piles of discarded shoes and clothes that were mildewed and damp. I passed them all, looking in as I went with the aid of the lantern. They were familiar and still strange which was why I liked being there.

Apart from the Library and my room at the top of the Very Tall House Near The Square, the Errid Shelter was one of my favourite places. The others were Sam Hall's bedroom; the Waiting Bench and a field on Whelme with a wood at my back.

AT THE LIBRARY

When I emerged from the Errid Shelter I was at the Library and Faer rain was falling in large soft and warm drops from a single cloud. I ran round its edges, across the terraces and up the steps until I came to the great revolving door. I pushed it around, enjoying its weight, and then I was inside the Library at the Reception and the Library's front desk.

When I arrived there aüggie was quite busy. Dane Margaret had a deposit to make and because she was quite particular about her deposits I could see that aüggie thought he had better pay attention.

First he made entries in the columns of the Bringing-In Book. He wrote carefully in his spider-blue ink with his lips pursed in concentration.

Second he wrote the receipt.

Third he said: "So, Margaret, where are we to deposit this now? Would you like to look at the Catalogue to help you decide?"

When Dane Margaret said that she thought that she would, aüggie led her across the hall to the lectern where the Catalogue was chained to the wood. As Margaret started to look through it aüggie turned to me. "Sorry to keep you, Issy," he said.

"That's all right," I told him. "I'm not in a hurry."

While I wait for aüggie and Dane Margaret I should tell you that the Library's front desk is not what you'd think. At least, it wasn't on that day and hasn't been since, from the time I am telling.

No, the front desk is long and smooth and made of wood that has been polished by all the deposits passing along it. Near the floor there is a brass rail to rest a foot upon while you wait. Unless there is a deposit waiting, the front desk is kept empty and clear. aüggie kept the Bringing-In Book beneath it on a shelf.

Around the front desk the hall is tall and cool with its high-vaulted windows and a view of the sea. The floor is marble and as flat as an iron except for the crack near the door. The best thing to do is to stride over the crack quickly and then pretend it's not there, which is what I had done.

I should tell about aüggie, too. He had not a tooth in his head and his yellow hair hung like thatch to his eyebrows as if it was hay. I would not have been surprised to see a sparrow fly out from beneath it.

THERE

By now Margaret and aüggie had found the correct page of the Catalogue and Margaret was happy. She returned to the front desk and carried her deposit away down the hall on the pads of her bare feet.

"There," aüggie told me. "That wasn't as bad as I thought it might be. Just let me tidy up here and we can take some rain cordial in the back office. Looks like we had just enough for two. I hope it don't get no busier today."

In the back office, which was the place where aüggie did his paperwork, he checked the pipe where the rain water ran in to mix with the cordial in the glass bottle shaped like a pear. He swirled it round a little and sniffed, then seemed satisfied.

"Let's drink cordial," he said.

DRINKING CORDIAL

We sat and drank our cordial. It was mint, of which I am not overly fond, but since it was aüggie I didn't say so. The deck chair was comfortable and it was good to sit down for a while.

"That friend of yours has been here," aüggie said after a time. "Came yesterday about half afternoon. Looked like he'd come from the River. His feet was all wet."

When he said that I knew who he meant. "You mean Patrice," I told him. "I wouldn't call him a friend."

"Oh? What would you call him?" aüggie asked.

"I'm not sure I'd call him anything yet. I'm not sure I like him that well."

"Well, whatever you'd call him, he was here till his feet were pretty much dry. Asked me if he could come back and I said: 'Sure, any time. Place is here, that's what it's for. Come back when you like.' He seemed okay with that."

"Did he talk about numbers?" I asked him.

"Funny you should say that," aüggie told me. "He didn't say nothing about numbers, but all day I've been seeing these numbers in chalk on shelves and on walls. Sometimes they're on doors or the floor. Damned if I know how they got there. Can't work it out. Coincidence, huh?"

"These things happen," I told him.

"So they tell me," he said. "Ain't never happened before, though. That's the odd thing."

We talked some more for a while, but not about numbers. I told aüggie about the Tea Dance. "I'm sorry you don't have an invitation," I said.

"I'm not," aüggie said. "The amount of work I got these days, if I took time out for a Tea Dance I'd never get back on schedule. People don't realise. People think this place'd run itself, I wasn't here."

I nodded because I could tell he was right. There have to be priorities. Then I remembered why I had come there.

"My father has Gone," I told aüggie. "He asked me to make a deposit but I don't have it with me. I'll bring it along later if that is all right."

"That's fine and handy with me," aüggie said. "I appreciate the notice, specially when it's busy, like today."

He sipped the last of his cordial and smacked his lips. "Ah," he said. Then: "Finally Gone then. Huh."

"Finally Gone," I told him and I felt a little of the nice feeling that was left from being with Sam Hall slip away.

"So, you going to be looking today?" aüggie asked me. "Or just passing through?"

He stood up so I knew it was time for him to get back to work. I set my glass on his desk.

"I think I'm just passing through today," I told him. "Now that I've told you about the deposit."

"Nice to see you again, Issy," he said. "Don't be a stranger, you hear?"

I told him I wouldn't.

I RETURN TO THE SIISTERS

When I returned to the Very Tall House Near The Square I found the Siisters were dozing in the Tea Room. Elaine was in her favourite deck chair with the blue and white stripes so I knew she felt good. Simone nodded on the stool at the counter and woke up when I entered.

"Hello, Issy," she said. "How did you get on? We expected you back before now."

I told Simone that I had got on very well. I told her that I had delivered all the invitations and also some of the things people had said when they had received them. Then I remembered to tell her that Sam Hall wished to send his regrets. He would be unable to attend the Tea Dance on account of his garden.

I had thought that Simone might be disappointed and for a moment she seemed so. Then she said: "Gardens are a true responsibility. I understand. We haven't seen Sam Hall in a long time so his garden must be a lot of work."

I told her that it was but that it was very beautiful because he worked so hard at it. I told her that the dirt was so fine and dark and smooth that it was like dipping your hands into a quince when you drew out the growing plants.

"Have you done the rubbing of the bodies thing with Sam Hall yet?" Simone asked me after I'd talked about drawing out the lettuce and carrots.

I told her I had.

"That's good," she said, nodding. "Sam Hall has a good body to rub with. It's like a stick."

I said I knew that and I thought so too.

"It's a shame Sam Hall cannot come," Simone said then. "If we are to keep our numbers correct we shall have to ask somebody else. I have thought about Simian fisher recently. Perhaps we should ask him."

"I'm sure he would be pleased to be asked," I said.

Simone nodded. "I think I shall talk about it with Elaine when she wakes up. Thank you, Issy," she said. "You have done a good job with the invitations. Things are looking up."

DREAMS OF PIES

Every night now the Siisters dreamed of new recipes. In the morning they wrote them down in a book. Sometimes it seemed that dozens had come in the night and I hoped there wouldn't be any Arrivals before the Tea Dance was over because I couldn't see how the Siisters would have space in their dreams for Arrivals, what with so many recipes to dream of and all.

Once they had written the dream-recipes down in the book the Siisters would pore over each one in intricate detail. They drank tea while they did this and sometimes ate toast, discussing ingredients and proportions and how each one would blend with the other. They always waited until the Tea Room was empty before they did this. They didn't want anyone hearing what things they might make for the Tea Dance before the Tea Dance began and they could see for themselves.

Sometimes a recipe would be discarded and sometimes a new one would be tested. Sometimes the smell of baking or basting that came from the kitchen would pull your nose in two or three different directions at once and there was no way to tell whether the mackerel and the strawberry sugar cream would be partnered together in a mackerel-strawberry sugar cream pie or held apart from each other like old friends who had fallen out about something some time ago and no longer spoke.

Because they were concentrating on their new recipes the Siisters had no time for small talk, except to say, "Issy, would you find us this or that thing from one place or another, but make sure it's firm and just ripe."

I didn't take any notice if they forgot to say "Please, Issy" because I knew how much the Tea Dance meant to them. I was glad to be asked to go in search of constance ham or wet onion, especially if the Siisters hadn't dreamed of precisely the same type of ham or the same number of wet onions. At moments like that they could be quite short with each other and I found it best to stay out of the way.

OUT OF THE WAY

During the days when I was staying out of the way, or while I was going off in search of something the Siisters had asked for, I started to notice numbers.

At the Watercress Beds I saw numbers written small and grey against the winding mechanism for the water pipes.

At Hog Field I saw numbers were written on thin strips of paper which fluttered from pins in the fence posts. One number was written on paper as long as my arm.

At the Nine Maidens (where the Siisters hadn't sent me, but where I had gone to stay out of the way of a disagreement about cheese) the numbers were made up of knots in a piece of string: two knots, then a space, then six knots, then a space, then two knots again. This was when I realised who had left these numbers and knew it was Patrice.

Patrice had been everywhere. I didn't know how he had done it. On the path to the Errid Shelter one of his numbers was made from pebbles in small heaps. Another was in a minute pile of sand so small that I had to squint closely to see it, but I knew that Patrice must have counted each grain of sand. This was on the steps to the Waiting Room near Fryst bridge.

Sometimes the numbers made sense straight away. Sometimes they only made sense after I had looked around for a long time and counted a lot of things that weren't right until I counted what was. Sometimes the numbers didn't make sense at all. Why was there a 17 made in feathers at Fairmile, or a 271 at Poorend Stand? I wondered if it had been the number of crows Patrice had seen when he stood there; or the number of seeds on a daisy head by his foot. I had no way to know.

At the primrose stile (as I was going to the watercress beds for a second time) I found Tilly looking at a number which was made of sticks poked into the earth. It was | | | | | | |.

"Hello, Issy," Tilly said. "What do you make of that?"

"I think it may be a number," I said. "214."

"Really?"

"I think so," I said.

"That's a strange number," Tilly said.

I have always liked Tilly quite well. She is tall and quite thin with a little grey hair and burnished brass spectacles on her nose. I know that my father liked her quite well too. Sometimes he would leave Fryst and come to Faer so they could walk the hill paths together. He would usually return with leaves in his clothes after this and when he found one he would smile and say, "That Tilly. I don't know."

"What could it be the number of, do you think?" Tilly asked then.

"I wouldn't like to guess," I said. I thought that 214 was rather a large number. I didn't want to start counting roof tiles on the falling down barn or rose hips on the bushes. I was getting wise to Patrice by now.

"If I'm not wrong there would seem to be four different ways in which the number may be read: 214; 2-14; 21-4; 2-1-4," Tilly said. "The problem is, we lack context."

"I think the context may be Patrice," I told her. "He is a prodigy with numbers but you may not have met him yet. He Arrived only recently."

"Is he a boy who looks like a chilly morning on Hallows when you're about to pick apples?" Tilly asked.

I said I thought that was a good description of Patrice.

"Ah, then I have met him," she said. "As a matter of fact we had quite a long conversation."

TILLY'S CONVERSATION WITH PATRICE

Tilly makes Works on the shore. She is prolific.

Some Works cannot be made just anywhere. Some can only be made in a place that is right. That was what my father had said when he told me we were going to live on Fryst for a while. He needed the cold to make the things he was working on, which turned out to be metanisms, although he didn't know that then.

Tilly makes her Works in the sand between tides. They require the ebb and the influx of the water to exist. Without that they would be nothing. These Works of Tilly's can not live in the Library either, but each time she makes one Tilly will go to the library (if she is satisfied) and tell aüggie about it. He will then enter it in the Catalogue so that we all know, if we care to look.

Tilly was at work on the shore when she saw Patrice, she told me. He was staring from the shore out to sea at the Off is-Lands with the look of someone who is trying to figure out where a sound has come from after it's stopped.

She engaged him in a conversation which began with "Hello, are you new here?" and ended with "Don't let me stop you".

In between they spoke about sand; water; wood; apples; a boat; Tilly's rake; a purple and yellow flower nearby; numbers; thinking; being busy; shoes; the is-lands; Wendell and sheep (how many).

While Tilly was having this intercourse with Patrice he had a branch of sweet amelia in his hand and he was carving a small piece of it with a knife shaped like a thorn. He carved the wood hard, like he was cutting off parts of himself with each stroke, Tilly observed.

She asked him what he was carving.

"Pegs for knot holes."

She asked if he would like to ask her a question.

Patrice said: "By the washing rock on Hallows there is a wasp made of twisted wire and straw. It hangs on a chain from the oak tree there. It is quite large."

Tilly nodded and said that she knew it.

"Is that a Work?" Patrice asked.

Tilly said that it surely was and that she thought it was very fine.

"But if it is a Work does that mean that all the Works are not in the library?" Patrice asked.

This was where Tilly explained the matter of some Works being in the Library and some not.

Patrice thought about that for a while. In the end he said: "That is interesting. It is not what I thought you would say."

Shortly afterwards Tilly told him that she ought to get back to the thing she had been doing before they had started their conversation.

"Don't let me stop you," Patrice told her.

That was the end of their conversation. It was nearly the end of my conversation with Tilly, also. I left her shortly thereafter.

THE OFF IS-LANDS

One morning the Siisters asked if I would find them some coast sloes for jam. They said that the sloes must have a good dusting of salt – they were very insistent on that – but they also said "please".

I knew just the right place for coast sloes with plenty of salt so I said: "I'll be happy to do that. May I borrow the water clock, please?"

I will explain the water clock in a moment.

I took a collecting tin with a lid as well as the water clock and a ball of string from behind the counter of the Tea Room, and while I set out to find sloes I will tell about the Off is-Lands.

We lived in the Far Lands, as I've already said. There are four is-lands that I have already mentioned: Faer and Fryst, Hallows and Whelme. What I haven't told yet is that there are far more is-lands than this, all different in size; from as big as a room to as long as a half-hour's walk in bare feet.

These other is-lands are the Off is-Lands which are all uninhabited, although many have names and on some you can find signs that they may once have been lived on, even though they no longer are.

The reason for this (no longer being lived on) is that the Off is-Lands cannot be predicted. You may think that you are walking on Huish when in fact you come back from Gugh. And if you take a canteen of water along you may find you aren't thirsty until it is gone; or that you never feel thirsty no matter how long you carry it in case you are dry.

These are just small things you might think, but there are other ways in which the Off is-Lands cannot be relied upon, and some are more unreliable than others. On these you might spend an hour gathering coast sloes but return a week after the Siisters had told you they wanted to make jam.

Alternatively, you might gather your sloes in your tin and return to the Tea Room before the Siisters have even dreamed of putting coast sloe jam in a cake. It is perfectly possible, also, that just as you are about to set off looking for coast sloes you might meet an Issy already returning with a full pound in her tin.

Any of these situations can have a confusing effect – as I'm sure you can imagine. If you can't I will tell you Francis's story.

FRANCIS'S STORY

Before I was old enough to remember, Francis Daychild was plaiting straw one afternoon as he waited for a stew on the fire. When he looked up to see how the stew was cooking he saw himself – as he later found out – returning from Litla Dimun with a cleft stick in his hand.

This was odd, not least because (as Francis would tell you) he had never had any intention of ever going to an Off is-Land in his life. But there he was, coming back from Litla Dimun and saying how that had been the best morning's walk of his life. He also wanted to know how it was that Francis was sitting on the stoop of *his* cabin, cooking *his* stew.

Of course, it didn't take too long for the Francises to figure out what had happened. Litla Dimun was known to be an Off is-Land with little regard for keeping things straight, so of course the Francises knew that one or other of them was in the wrong place. What they couldn't agree on, however, was which one of them it was.

Things were not helped by the fact that each Francis was exactly as stubborn as the other and neither was willing to give ground. So they fought, each and every day, over who sat in a chair or laid in the bed or cooked a meal or chopped wood or broke a fart. It was quite common for anyone who passed their cabin to see a Francis sporting a black eye or a bandage or walking with a limp.

Sometimes people would see a Francis crouched behind a wall or concealed in a thicket as they passed. If they spoke to say "Good morning, Francis" he would put a finger to his lips and say "Ssh! I'm waiting for the other one so I can hit him, the scrawny old bastard."

This situation lasted for several months: so long that people began to worry that one day one Francis would kill the other and no-one would know whether it was murder or suicide.

Finally, though – after one particularly bad fight in which one Francis was kicked in the shins and the other was knocked on the head with a stick – one Francis decided he couldn't stand it any more. He left the cabin early one morning and went off to Litla Dimun because he couldn't think of any other thing to do, although he'd never had any intention of going there in his life before.

There is only one Francis Daychild now and if you ask him he will tell you that the months of living with himself were the longest months of his life. He will also tell you that he has no desire to repeat the experience, which my father said was ironic because no-one he knew of had any desire to live with either Francis, either.

ON HUISH

So, by the time I've told this – about the Off is-Lands and Francis – I had come to ap-Huish Beach, which is the closest place to Huish that is still part of Faer is-Land. Huish was where I knew the coast sloes would be good and dusted with plenty of salt. Off is-Land sloes are the best if you require salt.

I set the water clock down on a rock and made sure it was full, then I tied one end of my string to a rusted metal ring set into a boulder. I tied the other end of the string to my finger. Then I hitched up my skirt and waded out towards Huish which is long and low and combed with sea-grass dunes.

The water was deep enough to reach to my thighs but underfoot the sand was rippled and smooth, rippled and smooth, without rocks. The water was also quite warm so it was a pleasant experience to wade slowly across the divide, holding my collecting tin clear of the brine.

When I reached the other side and waded out of the water on Huish I was pleased to see that the coast sloes there had as good a dusting of salt as I had hoped. I set to work picking them right away. They made a nice, round sound when they hit the bottom of the collecting tin.

THE NEARLY BOAT

While I was collecting the coast sloes I never went further than the length of the string tied to my finger and to the rusted ring on the opposite shore would allow. I went as far as I could to my right and when the string pulled tight I went back the other way. When the collecting tin was nearly full I saw a small boat up-turned in the sea-grass.

At first I was worried when I saw the boat. I thought that there might have been an Arrival that the Siisters hadn't dreamed of because their dreams were too full of recipes. Then I remembered that there could not have been an Arrival because Arrivals do not happen on Off is-Lands like Huish. Most often they happen on Faer, although sometimes they happen on Hallows or Whelme or Fryst, but they always happen on the inhabited is-lands. So I realised that the boat was not from an Arrival and I was glad about that.

When I went closer to the boat I could also see that it was in a poor shape. There were several knot holes in its planks and although one or two had been plugged with carved pegs and sealed up with wax, several more had not.

I looked at the boat for some time. It was a strange thing to see. I thought it looked either hidden or waiting but it was hard to tell which.

After I'd looked at the boat for a while I collected more coast sloes amongst the thin, tussocky sea-grass and put them in the tin. When I had enough I went back to the beach and followed the string, winding it in as I waded back to the opposite shore. That was where I saw Patrice again.

PATRICE AGAIN

Patrice was standing on the shore near the water clock as I stepped out of the sea and on to the beach. When I looked at the water clock I could tell how long I had been gone and it was only long enough to collect a tin full of coast sloes and look at a boat, so I was glad about that. I was glad I wouldn't be meeting another Issy on her way out to collect coast sloes with a good dusting of salt.

"Good morning, Patrice," I said. Now that I'd looked at the water clock I had decided to be friendly again. I said: "Are you well? How did you cut your head?"

"I don't know yet," he said, putting a delicate finger to the cut on his head. "I can't tell."

"Ah," I said.

"What were you doing?" he asked then.

I told him that I had collected coast sloes for the Siisters who might or might not make jam for the Tea Dance. I showed him the tin.

"I don't understand," he said then. "Is there going to be another Tea Dance?"

"I don't know that there will be another," I said. "I think the Siisters will wait to see how the first one turns out."

Patrice frowned when I said that. He looked like a person who has misplaced their pencil without having moved.

Then I noticed his wet shoes and trousers. "Have you been standing in the River?" I asked him.

"Not for a long time," he said.

"Your trousers are wet."

He looked down. "So they are," he said. "I'm not sure how that happened. I'm not sure about several things. I have tried to make sense of it all with the right numbers but I think it has made things harder, not better."

"I thought you knew all the numbers," I said. "I thought you are a prodigy."

Patrice shook his head. "I don't think any of my numbers were the right numbers," he said. "I have had second thoughts since we met at the Library."

He looked away from me then and I could see that he was ashamed of something. I couldn't tell what it was, though.

"We haven't met at the Library," I told him. "But aüggie tells me you've been there. He's quite perplexed by the numbers you've left."

"I'm sure I haven't left any numbers," Patrice said. "I've thought a great many, but I haven't left them behind."

"Oh," I said. "That's strange. I've found your numbers elsewhere as well."

"Are you sure they are mine?"

"They look very like yours," I told him. "I don't think they could be anyone else's."

Patrice shook his head. "I don't recall them," he said. "Not a one or a seven or a ten."

"Oh," I said.

This was becoming very unsettling.

ASKED AND ANSWERED

I had come to like Patrice better by now. I thought that I might have misjudged him before. He was different to the time he had stood by the river and told me my numbers.

"May I ask you a question," I said then.

"Of course, go ahead," he said. He sat down on the sand facing me. He had his knees drawn up to is chin.

"How many times have we met? Can you say?"

"Including today?"

"Not including today."

"Three," Patrice said without hesitation. "Once at the Arrival. Once at Wendell's Place when we walked to the River. Once at the Library."

"Hmm," I said. "May I ask you something else?"

"Of course. This is very interesting."

"How long ago is it since we met at the Library?" I asked. I knew that we had not met at the Library, but I wanted to see what Patrice would say.

He thought quite hard. "I would say it was at least sixteen days. It's hard to be sure. I think I've lost count."

He shook his head as he said this and I saw that there was a redness on his neck, like an graze that was fading. The marks looked like a band of leaves round his throat.

"How did you get here?" I asked. "To this place, now. Where did you come *from*?"

Patrice frowned at the question and put a finger to the cut on his head again. He touched it less delicately this time. "I think I have been in a boat," he said in the end. "That is all I can think of. I think I was *put* in a boat and then put out of it. That is all I can think of."

"The nearly boat?" I asked.

"What is the nearly boat?"

"I don't know if that is really what it would be called," I said. "It is just what I called it because it is not quite a boat. It is out there on Huish, amongst the dunes. At least, it was. It may not be now. You never can tell. I thought it might be a Work, but it might not."

"It's on the is-land?" Patrice asked looking at Huish across the water.

"Yes," I told him.

"Perhaps I should go take a look," he said.

"That might be a good idea," I said. I thought I knew what might have happened now. "But before you do, have you heard the story of Francis and Francis?"

When I said this Patrice looked at me sharply. "That is the same question you asked at the Library," he said.

"I thought it might be," I said. "And what did you say?"

"I said that I hadn't. You refused to tell me what it was."

"I will tell you now," I said.

That was when I told Patrice the story of Francis and Francis.

I WILL NOT WAIT

After I had told Patrice the story of Francis and Francis he thought for quite some time. I was not surprised by that and I waited for him to finish.

"Am I different?" he asked then.

"I believe so," I said. "I like you better than I did."

Patrice thought about that, too. "If I am the same me I'm glad," he said then. "But I think I am not."

"I believe it is too soon to tell," I told him. "It can be confusing."

He nodded. "I understand if you do not wish to mention it," he said after he had looked away and then back. "But I'm sorry that it happened that way. I know it will be no consolation, but I wish I could undo what I did. I do not feel the same way any more."

I stood up. (I had sat down on the dry sand some time before.)

"I will not wait," I told Patrice. "But I will leave the water clock and string if you like."

"Thank you, Issy," Patrice said. "I'm glad that you like me better than before."

I smiled at him to show that we were friends now and then I set off towards Town. (I remembered to take the collecting tin full of coast sloes.)

I looked back from the top of a sand dune, just before the beach would disappear from sight, but I couldn't see Patrice any more. On the far side of the water on Huish an old woman in a check shawl raised a hand to me and waved. I waved back. She looked familiar, I thought.

AN ARRANGEMENT FOR NETS

While I'd been gone the Siisters had been to the harbour to see Simian fisher. They asked if they could borrow some of his nets to hang from the trees.

Simian's nets were a wonder. When he hauled them from the water they became full, pregnant bellies of silver writhing fish which had come to admire themselves in the mirrors and sequins which Simian sewed into his nets. This was the secret of Simian's success as a fisher. No-one else sewed mirrors and sequins the way he did. No-one else smelled of fish the same way, either.

When the Siisters asked him if they could borrow some nets Simian said he didn't see why he should help them out seeing as how *he* hadn't been invited to the Tea Dance. He was sore about that.

"We considered inviting you," Elaine told him. "But as you never come to the Tea Room we assumed that you wouldn't want to come to a Tea *Dance*."

"I might come to the Tea Room," Simian said. "If it wasn't for that fucking gate always biting me. A man doesn't want to drink tea and look at cakes when he's been bitten by a fucking gate. He'd rather go someplace else and drink cider."

Elaine and Simone looked at each other after he said this. They had needs and they thought that Simian fisher might want to attend to them if it wasn't for the fucking gate.

"Perhaps we can come to an arrangement," Simone said. "Perhaps you might use the front door instead of the gate and the steps."

She looked to see if Elaine was on the same wavelength even though she knew that she would be.

"I think we could let you do that," Elaine said. "It wouldn't do for everyone, but we can see that being bitten by that gate might put you out of a mood to drink tea and look at cakes and that is a shame."

"I can be discreet," Simian told them. "I don't need to tell no-one else about the front door. I haven't drunk tea in an age."

"Would you like to walk out to the end of the quay with us?" Simone asked. "We can speak about nets."

"Sure," Simian told them. "Why not?"

He put away his needle and mirrors.

By the time the Siisters had returned from the walk to the end of the quay with Simian it was settled. They all smelled vaguely of fish. That was when I returned from collecting the coast sloes and when I remarked on their scent they told me about Simian and the nets.

THE SMELL OF FISH

A few days later Simian brought the nets as they had arranged and we all hung them from the branches of the trees in the garden. The mirrors and sequins and fish scales really did look very interesting. Afterwards Simian took tea and looked at cakes, though he didn't eat any.

The following afternoon the Siisters and I stretched a large piece of burgundy canvas as tight as a drum beneath the nets. We pegged it down with short wooden spikes made from hazel so that it would stay nice and taut across the lawn and make a good surface for dancing.

Elaine and I did a short waltz on the canvas to try it for size. Then we stood in the centre of the canvas and looked up at the mirrors in the nets. I said I was sure it would be just right for dancing but I was concerned about the smell of fish from the nets. I wondered if it might distract people from their cake.

When I said this Elaine told me she was confident that the aroma would be much less noticeable by the time of the Tea Dance.

I still wasn't sure. I would have asked Simone what she thought about this but I couldn't do that. While Elaine and I had danced and looked at the nets someone had rung the bell at the front door and Simone hadn't returned from answering it yet.

I wondered who the caller might be who didn't know that the way to find the Siisters was to come through the gate and down the granite steps to the Flying Horse Tea Rooms. Whoever it was was certainly taking their time to be told this. Simone had been gone for an hour.

When she returned I asked Simone about the smell of the nets. She said she was coming round to the aroma of fish. She didn't think it would distract from the cakes.

THE DAY BEFORE THE TEA DANCE

It was now the day before the day of the Tea Dance and I knew there was something else I must do, which was to visit the

Library again. It had been on my mind even while we had hung the nets from the trees and I thought I should do it now before preparations for the Tea Dance became too advanced.

When I told Simone where I would be going she nodded, of course. Upstairs the front doorbell had rung again and Elaine was busy answering it. Simone suggested I leave by the steps.

LIKE A DOG

It was an Exchange & Mart Day in the Square and as I passed by – though I didn't stop to look or exchange with anyone because I had somewhere to be – I heard several people mention a name.

The name was Patrice, and I could tell that they were saying it in a way that was either puzzled or resentful. The way I heard it they would say his name and then talk about numbers and I thought I knew what that meant. I thought that the people who spoke of it had found numbers in places where Patrice had been, and in 1 or 2 cases Patrice had spoken to people and told them numbers directly. Then it would depend on the person whether they liked that or not, or perhaps did not understand.

I thought about this as I passed the Square and took the road to the Library. I wondered if Patrice knew what he was doing.

To reach the Library from the Town you must walk as if you are going to Whelme, but then not. At the fork in the road you go left towards the gorse on the hill. If there is a breeze from that direction you can smell the heady yellow smell of the gorse a long time before you come to it and must follow the narrow sandy paths between the spikes of the bushes.

I was walking these paths when I saw Patrice. He did not see me. He was ahead on the path, going towards the Library like a dog intent on a scent. I have never seen a dog because there are none on the is-lands, but Patrice looked like I imagined a dog would look just before he disappeared from sight over the brow of the hill.

THE STANDING AND RESTING PLACES

When you have walked along the gorse path and followed it uphill you will come to the Standing Place. There you will probably stop and stand, or you can sit down if you wish. There is a seat there. It is two pieces of granite stone, one in front of the other. The stone at the front is the seat, the one at the back is the back.

You can sit there on the seat and lean back and rest. It is the Resting Seat and there is a small sandy patch of ground in front of it where people's feet have rested and worn away the grass. To rest there for five minutes feels as if you have rested for an hour, perhaps more. The more weary you are the greater the feeling. That is what the Resting Seat does. I have a feeling that it may have been made by the same person who made the Waiting Bench at the harbour, but there is no way to tell.

I did not rest on the seat because I wasn't in need. I did stand at the Standing Place, however, and I looked down on the Library and followed the steps to its door with my eyes.

From the Standing Place it is clear that the Library grows out of the hillside and hangs over the cliff. It has walls the colour of chalk that have no lines or cracks but are smooth and angular and sweeping. There is far more to the Library than you can see from the Standing Place. From there you cannot see the terraces and steps, the galleries or the halls. You can only see the entrance and a part of the entrance hall.

To see more you must go inside. Then, from the windows on the inside, you can see out across the ocean as far as the horizon with nothing between. The Library is our World's End, and that's as it should be.

THE CRACK

Inside the Library I stepped over the crack in the marble floor and pretended it wasn't there, even though I thought it looked longer and wider than the last time I had pretended the same thing. I was alone at the front desk until aüggie heard my polite cough and came out of his office.

"Hello, Issy," he said. "Was that you running past here just a few minutes ago?"

"I haven't run," I told aüggie. "I only just walked in."

"Hmm," aüggie said. "I'm pretty sure I heard someone running."

"I think the person running might have been Patrice," I told him. "He was headed this way like a dog on a scent."

When I said this aüggie nodded as if that made sense. "That one's a strange one," he said. "He's in and out like a toad. And when he's not in and out he's here without ever leaving."

"That is strange," I said. "What does he do?"

aüggie told me that Patrice would spend the days searching amongst the rooms. "Searching" was the word aüggie used to describe it.

"Like he's looking for something," he told me. "Like he knows what it isn't. Like he can touch something, smell something, look at something and know it's not what he's after, but he knows he'll know what it is when he finds it."

Sometimes, aüggie said, he would find Patrice asleep on a cot in a hall or catch sight of him taking a drink from a tap in the lobbies. "God knows what he eats," aüggie said. "I've never seen him eat. There's nothing to eat here."

"Does he speak?" I asked then.

"He speaks sometimes," aüggie said. "Sometimes he doesn't. I asked if he wanted a Library card but he told me he didn't. Said he wasn't going to be around long enough to make it worth filling out all those forms."

"How many forms are there?" I said.

"Just the one: Name and number."

I nodded. I remembered that was true because there had been a problem when I first wanted to join the Library. My name is Issy (which is short for Isadora) but because I was born on the is-lands and did not Arrive, I have no number.

For a while it was a difficult thing to resolve, how I would join the Library, but in the end aüggie said that for me he would make an exception, being as how he knew me and all.

"Perhaps Patrice didn't want us to know his number," I suggested. "We know his name, but perhaps he prefers to keep his number to himself."

Now aüggie nodded. "That would be a reason," he said. "Pity he don't keep his other numbers to himself. He has enough of them for three."

I nodded and said I thought that he had.

"So what about you, Issy?" aüggie went on. "Are you making a deposit today? Did you bring that Work of your father's you mentioned before?"

"Not this time," I told him. "I think I came here to meet Patrice, so I had better get to it."

"I guess you had, then," aüggie said. "Don't let me hold you up."

As I moved to enter the Library I had a second thought. I turned back to aüggie.

"I don't like to mention it," I said. "But the crack by the door; I think it has grown larger."

We both didn't look at the crack but aüggie nodded. "I'm sure you are right," he said. "I noticed it, too."

"Do you think it means something?" I asked.

"Hard to tell without looking," aüggie told me. "Best way I figure it, it's some kind of settlement. Least, I hope that's what it is."

We didn't look towards the crack for a moment longer and then aüggie went back to his office and I started down the hallway, into the Library.

HALLS & ROOMS

I cannot tell you how wonderful the Library is. I could try and maybe I will, but it will not be a fraction of a fraction of what you would have seen if you had been there.

The Library was a place to get lost in. Like the is-lands there were no maps of the Library, and if there had been they would have been useless. You could get lost in the halls, or the rooms or the shelves or the cases. You would turn a corner and enter a gallery and before you knew it you would have stepped far and wide of where you began.

Some galleries were so long you could not walk the rush mats down their centre from one end to the other in less than half an hour. Very often you would stop by a high window and look out across the blue ocean and the high, balloon clouds before turning back and encountering a Work suspended by silk.

Part way along a gallery you might find a plank and board door with a blackwork latch, and beyond it – inside it – the room would swallow you into its panels and pine floorboards as you came to the smallest of shelves without drawers, upon and within which there would be a red thread and a pin.

In a room called *Constant* you would find a glass dish, half full of water and on it – floating in a small metal boat, a candle.

Next to the glass dish there would be a box of matches and you would know that if you struck one and applied the flame to the candle there would be something to see, there in front of you. Then you would decide whether or not to light the candle before you moved on.

In one hall, called *Departures*, there was a wall made entirely of suitcases, each with a label. Some of the labels were written in childish letters, some were written in beetle-ish ink or in pencil. Some would say "Property Of...." and others would be written with a message in case the suitcase was lost and a person found it and wanted to return it but didn't know how. One of the labels said *"Take what you want. I don't care any more."* It was written in green ink and there was a water stain in the corner.

There is a room full of water, called *Thirst*; there is a room with dried skins and bladders; there is a room of sticks and another of stairs. There is a room called *Eyed* which makes you feel cold.

One of my favourite rooms – when I could find it – was the room called *Snug*. I liked the fact that the room smelled of pipe tobacco and the red leather upholstery. On a very long, very narrow table down the centre of the room were a series of brass and glass things, some with cogs and ratchets for adjustment, others just as simple as they could be.

At the far end of the table, where it met the wall, there was a small tear-shaped plate of brass affixed by a screw. If you swung the brass plate aside a narrow beam of light from the outside somewhere would shine down the length of the table through the glass and the   brass.

COUNTLESS

If I told of all the rooms and the things within them here I would never reach the end. It would be impossible. Even the catalogue at the front desk had a hundred earlier volumes, stored in a room adjacent to aüggie's office called *Catalogue*. No-one, not even aüggie, could tell how many items they listed. You could lose yourself for a day just looking up the word *water*, which you would think would be a simple thing but is anything but. I know because I have done it.

It is very easy to lose yourself in the Library unless you have purpose and determination. Even then it is still easy. I will often take a sandwich if I am going into the Library because – as aüggie had said – there is nothing to eat there, although there are taps in some of the halls.

2

When I saw Patrice he was coming from *Stones* and when he saw me he turned away. He was half turned away and I saw him put something in his pocket before he turned back again and continued towards me.

"Hello, Patrice," I said. "What had you got there?"

"Nothing," he said, but we knew he was lying. When he knew that I knew he said: "77."

I blinked but said nothing.

"And 15," he said when he saw this. His voice was a scowl.

"Your numbers don't frighten me," I said. "I have seen them a lot now. They are becoming familiar. In fact I discussed them with Tilly. She told me about your long conversation."

"I don't know any Tilly," he said.

"2," I said.

"2 what?"

"2 untruths," I told him. "Don't you know?"

"I don't care," he said, and I knew that was true.

"Patrice," I said. "You haven't been here very long. Perhaps you should give people more time before you tell them your numbers. I think some people find it unsettling."

"I can't help that," he said. "And they are *their* numbers, not mine. I have nothing to do with it."

"You have *something* to do with it," I said because it was true.

Patrice said nothing to that. Instead he turned and strode away down the hallway and as he did so I noticed that his shoes and the legs of his trousers were wet, as if he had been wading in the sea or standing in the River.

A MAP OF THE IS-LANDS

I waited a short while and then I followed Patrice's damp footprints along the hallway, past *Stories* and *Field*. At the end of the hall a small, carved door was open and inside it the footprints mounted a stair. I mounted it too and when I passed a window I knew I was in a tower because there was a view of the cliff and the white surf below.

After that there was a doorway, hung with a faded piece of sailcloth. This was not a place I had found in the Library before, but that's the way of it sometimes. I stepped into the room as Patrice took a stone from his pocket and placed it amongst an intricate collage of things which I knew he had brought there out of the galleries and rooms and the shelves.

When I saw these things laid out on the floor I knew what they were. Patrice had made a map of the is-Lands, although such a thing is not possible. I watched as he took the stone from his pocket and placed it in the place where I knew that Huish would be if a map of the is-Lands could be made that would hold still and be true.

"You have made a map," I said. "No-one I know of has ever made a map of the is-Lands before."

When I said it Patrice jumped and almost knocked the stone out of position. He turned to look at me.

"Why are you following me?" he demanded.

"I thought you might want the company," I told him. "I also wanted to ask you a question."

I took a step into the room so that I could see the map properly. It was a very intricate thing. It wove countless objects into a thing that was both disturbing and pretty.

The map was perfectly clear. I could see the Town and the Harbour, the Errid Shelter and the long field at Fairmile. If you looked closely you could see that none of these things were those things: they were something else entirely. But as you drew back your eye you could see that the map was entirely accurate, too. You just had to look at it right.

NOBODY KNOWS

"Does aüggie know about this?" I asked while I was still looking. I knew that Patrice was watching me as I looked.

"Nobody knows," Patrice told me. I could tell he was proud of what he had made.

"I'm not sure aüggie will be happy," I said. "He can be quite particular when he's in the mood."

"That doesn't matter to me," Patrice said then. "What matters is this. Soon it will add up and when it does I will leave. I'm almost done."

I stopped looking at the map then. I looked at Patrice instead. Now I understood the numbers I had been finding in different places. Each place with a number was a place on Patrice's map of the is-Lands.

"Patrice," I said gently. "You've only just Arrived here. I'm not sure it is possible to be here and Gone in such a short time."

"I have been here for months," he said. "And I hate it. And I said *leave* – I didn't say *Gone*. It wasn't my idea to come here. If you want to know who is responsible you should ask Martin and Dot."

"I couldn't do that. It is against the Rule."

"The Rule, the Rule," Patrice said as if it was a bad taste in his mouth.

I could tell now that now wasn't the time to pursue the matter any further. I could tell that Patrice was not in the mood for further discussion.

I said: "I had better go now. I expect the Siisters will be looking for help pretty soon."

I turned away.

"You said you wanted to ask me a question," Patrice said. "You haven't done that."

I remembered. I said: "Have you heard the story of Francis & Francis?"

Patrice shook his head. "No-one has mentioned it to me."

"I thought not," I said. "Goodbye, Patrice."

"Wait," he said then. "Tell me the story – if that's what you want."

I shook my head. "I don't think now is the time," I told him. "In fact I know it is not."

When I said this Patrice's brow darkened. "27," he said, and I knew that he meant it.

I was still for a moment, just a little bit sad, then I said: "Even if a number is true, that doesn't make it right."

Patrice stamped his foot. "You don't know everything," he said. "You know less than everyone else. You are the only one on the is-Lands who has never seen the Other Place. You don't know what it is like, but I think you *should* know."

"No thank you," I said. "I have no wish to know."

"Look," he said. "We are alone. I can say and do what I like. Who would stop me?"

"No-one," I said.

"So I could tell you about the Other Place. No-one would know."

"I would know," I told him. "Goodbye Patrice."

AS I TURNED FOR THE DOOR

As I turned for the door I heard Patrice's angry feet coming after me. I heard the scattering of objects which made up his map of the is-Lands. Then I felt his hand on my shoulder. I tried to shake it off but he took hold of my other shoulder, too, and from behind me I felt the damp of his breath as he pushed his face into the hair by my ear. Then he whispered. I did not move. I closed my eyes. I waited until he had finished and then I waited until he said, "There."

I did not move. I kept my eyes closed. I waited until he went away.

I STAY IN BED

When I returned to the Very Tall House I didn't notice the smell of fish at the front door or the sound of a broken picture inside the Siisters' room. I climbed the 77 steps to my own room and I went to bed in my clothes. I wanted to stay there for a long time, so I did. I lay under the eiderdown, very still. When it grew dark in the window I got out of the bed and took off my clothes, then I returned to lie under the quilt as still as before.

I was very unhappy.

Patrice had been right. It was no consolation.

IN THE DARK LANDS

TIN (SN)

Once a once a time there was a boy who was found amongst the ruins and rubble, as if he was hiding.

The boy would not speak and for many days he refused to open his eyes. The men who found him brought him out of the rubble to the sheds where the lights hung in straight lines. They told the Supervisor that when the boy was found his shoes were wet. "As if he'd been standing in a river."

The boy was well treated – as much as anyone was able. Although there were no other children in the sheds, a place was made for the boy. He was given a bed in a dormitory and when he opened his eyes he was shown around the camp. It was the most the Supervisor could do without further instructions, for the dispersal of lost children was not a high priority.

Because he would not speak, and because he showed little or no reaction to anything he saw, the Supervisor thought the boy might be simple. In order that he might have something to occupy himself, and also contribute to the work of the sheds, the boy was shown how to sweep up the tally chads and other simple tasks.

The boy accepted these instructions wordlessly and went to work in the same way.

SHED 3

Several weeks passed and the Supervisor still did not receive any instructions regarding the boy. However, it had been noticed that the boy had a facility for numbers which he could communicate with quick flicks of his fingers if he leaned his broom handle in the crook of his arm. Occasionally now he spoke also, although his voice was hoarse and staccato.

"He's a great counter," the shed foreman told the Supervisor. "We should move him to Shed 3 and let him do more."

So the boy was moved to the third shed and when they wanted to know the number of something they would ask the boy and he would tell them with his fingers or cracked voice, whether it was the number of shoes or pencils or people.

After a few weeks of this the boy started to do things differently. He would arrive at the shed earlier than the others and cut strips of paper with a knife. On these he wrote numbers which he passed out to the others as they arrived.

Sometimes the recipient of a slip would not understand and then the boy told them in his own stilted way what each number meant. Then the man or the woman would nod and say: "Ah, I got you." And they would set to work.

Soon, in this way, processing became faster and more efficient. Accuracy was improved and as a result there were times when the sheds finished work by mid-afternoon. Then the people all grinned at each other and said it was a fine thing to have no more work and be able to relax a little before the dinner bell rang. It was very fine, they said.

WHAT WILL BECOME OF HIM?

Months passed until one afternoon, just after lunch, a captain arrived at the camp. He had come to see how it was that these sheds beyond all the others in the arrondissement had become more efficient.

After a conversation with the Supervisor – which the Supervisor found unsettling because the captain gave nothing away – the visitor was taken to the boy who was counting and calculating in shed 3.

The captain watched this for a while, then he stepped forward and drew the boy away from the counting desk and sat him down in a corner. He spoke to the boy for several minutes and the boy replied in the stilted way he had of speaking, as if communicating in that manner was still an unfamiliar thing to him.

When he had finished speaking with the boy the captain requested the use of the telephone and was taken to the Supervisor's office with its plank walls painted white. It took some time for the connection to be made and the captain smoked while he waited.

Finally the captain emerged from the office and relayed his instructions to the shed Supervisor. The boy was brought out of shed 3 to the captain's waiting car. It was black and shiny, with running boards and a walnut facia. Its seats were upholstered in green leather.

"What will become of him?" the shed Supervisor asked as the boy was put in the back seat. He had become used to the boy's presence and had grown to rely on his accuracy.

The captain shrugged. "I only know what they tell me and that isn't much. Does he have belongings? I'd better take them, too, if he does."

The Supervisor sent a woman to the dormitory shed and when she returned with the boy's belongings these were given to him. Then the captain got into the front of the car alongside the driver and the Supervisor watched as the car drove away.

The sun was low in the sky and the cattle in the fields around the sheds had moved to chew the cud in the long shadows where the grass was still damp. It was a good evening, the Supervisor thought. It was a pity that the boy was no longer there to improve their accuracy.

(AND PENCILS)

The boy was taken to a new camp where the buildings still smelled of freshly planed wood and linseed oil from the putty around the window glass. The camp had been built on the site of an orchard and several apple trees still remained.

The work at this place was similar to the first camp, although not quite the same. The system of handing out numbered slips of paper to each worker as they arrived was now a standard practice, but the boy was no longer required to do this. Instead he was encouraged to observe other aspects of the sheds' work and assess them.

"See what you can do," the new Supervisor told him. "No pressure. We all hear you did great things at the last place you was at. We could use some of that."

The boy nodded silently to show that he understood and the Supervisor handed him a notebook and a new pencil. Then the boy crossed the shed to sit on a small stool in the corner and observe.

After a few days the Supervisor returned to the shed expecting to find the boy still observing, but the boy wasn't there. When the Supervisor asked about this he was told that the boy had not returned after the first day and no-one was sure where he had gone.

Hearing this the Supervisor became concerned. He was afraid of what might be said if the boy had been lost. He knew some would think his supervision had been inadequate, and his fears grew when he went to the dormitory. He was told that they boy had only slept two nights there immediately after his arrival and had not been seen since.

Sweating slightly, the Supervisor called together six men on whom he could rely and organised a search of the camp. Each shed and hut was to be checked and one man was sent off to inspect the storage bins a quarter of a mile down the track. It was a matter of urgency, the Supervisor told them. Things could depend on this.

As it turned out, however, things did not.

There was an unoccupied hut close to a playground at the south end of the camp. All this hut contained was a table – either lost or forgotten – and a carpenter's saw horse. This was where the boy was found about ten minutes after the search had begun.

When the Supervisor entered the hut he was relieved to see the boy quietly sitting on the saw horse, like a chair.

"You had us worried," the Supervisor told him. "Boy, you did."

Then he saw that the boy had separated the leaves of his notebook and spread them out over the table. Each page was filled with numbers. The new pencil was worn to a nub.

No-one at the camp was able to understand what the pages of numbers represented, or if they represented anything at all. The boy could not or would not explain.

This left the Supervisor with a conundrum. He had been given instructions regarding the boy, but they did not cover this eventuality, which had not been foreseen.

After some consultation with the shed foremen it was decided that the boy should be given as much paper (and pencils) as he required. It was also decided by a vote of the allocation subcommittee that he should be allowed to remain alone in the hut. It was an unusual thing, the Supervisor agreed, but he for one thought that it was better than the alternative, although he did not spell out what he thought the alternative might be.

Therefore a camp bed was installed in a corner of the unused hut: green tubular steel with a blue canvas stretcher. There were also two heavy woollen blankets and a pillow. A cardboard box containing paper and pencils was placed beside the table, on the floor, so the boy could take what he needed.

THE MAN IN GABARDINE AND SILK

From then on the boy rarely left the hut except to bathe in the washroom. Sometimes the other inhabitants of the camp would walk past and look in at the windows to see the boy standing perfectly still in the centre of the room. Sometimes at night, in the yellow cast of the lights, they would see him walking slowly in a circle around the table where his pieces of paper were laid out. Sometimes they would look and the windows would be dark and then they would know that the boy was asleep on the cot.

At the start of every month a skinny man dressed in gabardine and silk would arrive at the camp with a brown leather satchel. After speaking briefly with the Supervisor he would be escorted to the boy's hut and would knock at the door. When the boy opened it the man would enter and the door would be closed behind him.

No-one in the camp – not even the Supervisor – knew what passed between the boy and the man in gabardine and silk on these visits. It was clear that something did pass between them, however. Those who glanced in at the windows – and a glance was all they would risk if the man in gabardine was there – would often see the boy and the man sitting on Utility chairs facing each other, knees almost touching.

Sometimes the man would be looking at a sheet of yellow paper. Sometimes it seemed as if the boy was talking in his particular, stilted manner. Sometimes these meetings would last for an hour, sometimes for only a few minutes, and then the man would leave with papers in his satchel. Sometimes the man would leave something behind for the boy to consider.

Two and sometimes three times a year there would be an Errid warning and then the sheds would be closed and the people would file into the shelter and wait. At these times the Supervisor always made sure that he was close to the boy, for he knew that the boy might be uncomfortable amongst the others and he felt responsible for his well-being even though the boy asked for nothing.

DANDY

To the others in the camp the boy became known as *Torgben*, which means "yellow paper" and also "giver" to some.

One day in the yard the boy passed by as the children played a game with the windfall apples. They bowled an apple each as far as they could across the gritty, asphalt surface of the yard, each trying to out-do the others. When one succeeded in beating his peers a great cheer would go up and all would shout "Dandy!"

The boy – *Torgben* – was crossing the yard from the wash-house to his hut when he saw an unclaimed apple near the fence. He stopped there, then picked it up and handled its shape for a moment, as if calculating the irregularities and densities of its pith and skin.

"Bowl it!" one of the other boys called, seeing *Torgben* and his apple.

The boy hesitated for a moment. He had never been asked to participate in a game before. He assessed the vectors and curves for a moment, then threw the apple.

It arced high and clear. When it hit the ground with a thud it was already several yards beyond all the other apples on the asphalt and it continued to roll until it reached the redbrick wall.

The boy waited for the shout of "Dandy!" to go up from the others, but they remained silent.

"That doesn't count," the other boy said. "You have to throw under, not over."

The boy – *Torgben* – seemed puzzled by this.

"Let him take it again," a girl in a cotton dress said. The dress was pinned with pink flowers. "He didn't know that over doesn't count."

The boy – *Torgben* – turned away silently and started across the yard towards his hut. A moment later the girl ran after him and pressed an apple into his hand. She might have been two or three years younger than him.

"It was a good throw all the same," she said. "Even if it didn't count."

She smiled at him, just for a moment, and then she ran back to the others.

The boy took the apple she had given him back to the hut. He placed it at the centre of the long table there and would look at it once in a while between calculations. It remained there until its green-red had become brown and its skin had wrinkled to a quarter of its original size.

Sometimes in the morning he would find a fresh apple on the stoop when he left the hut to fetch a jug of water. Each time he stepped carefully over the offering and did not disturb it.

LEAVING THE HUT

And so the years passed and the boy – *Torgben* – grew to manhood. His hut no longer smelled of newly-planed wood and linseed but little else had changed. Each day he would apply himself to the calculations left by the man in gabardine and silk at the start of the month.

It was noted, however, that the young man would often stand at the west window of the hut and gaze out across the remains of the orchard towards the shifting plain of grass in the distance. At these times the young man had the look of someone who is trying to recall a dream they are not sure they have had.

Finally, one spring, the man in gabardine and silk arrived without his satchel.

He spoke with the Supervisor – a woman now, and not the same Supervisor who had held the post when the camp was new. The man in gabardine informed her that a decision had been reached.

Together they went to the boy's hut, although the boy – *Torgben* – was no longer a boy now, but a young man, much taller and slender with a serious face.

When they were inside the hut the man in gabardine told *Torgben* that arrangements had been made for a move to the city. The young man's work was considered too important to remain in the hut any longer. He would like the city, the man in gabardine said: he would have more opportunities there.

The young man said nothing for a time and then he agreed without speaking.

A short time later the young man left his hut with the man in gabardine and silk. The new Supervisor closed the door behind them. She watched as the young man walked to the car and realised that he was now a full head taller than the man who accompanied him. She did not have the same degree of fondness for the boy as her predecessor had had and she felt some relief when a number of men arrived to box up everything in the young man's hut and take it away.

IN THE CITY

The young man was given a pleasant if modest apartment on the sixth floor of a building which faced the afternoon sun. He was given an office in a building which had many offices and many people, some of whom would speak with each other, some of whom would not.

After a year the man in gabardine and silk came to see the young man in his office. It was as bare as the day the young man had first been shown in there. The pencils were untouched.

The man in gabardine saw this. He asked why.

"This place is not for me," the young man said. "I would like to return to the camp. I have tried to like it here and failed. May I go back to the hut?"

The man in gabardine told him that it was not his decision to make, but he would confer with others. Something would be decided.

A few days later the man in gabardine and silk returned. A decision had been made. He told the young man that he was to go north, to a plant in the province of K____. There his task would be to apply all his previous work and implement the processes he had already formulated while he had been in the camp. When the new work was complete there would be an inspection: an assessment of the success or otherwise of the project. It was anticipated that the project would take several years, the man in gabardine said.

The young man packed a bag and on the advice of the man in gabardine and silk he bought a new pair of boots before he left for the rail station. As he departed the city he felt great anticipation and relief that his confinement in the city was finally ending.

K____

The journey north took several days. The province of K____ was as isolated as it was barren, save for the plantations of trees which grew in thick squares, a mile on each side, and were harvested for fuel.

On the open plain the young man watched these plantations go by, with the cabins for the forestry workers standing neatly outside their boundary lines. But two days later even these had ceased.

On the final day of his journey the train made a wide, sweeping curve towards its destination and the young man saw his first view of the town, sitting at the base of the foothills of the Ghyll Mountains like a tussock of grass on the plain.

When he disembarked from the train he was the only passenger left. No-one else had come this far. The föhn wind was blowing warmly from the SE and the young man noticed a strange absence of sound in the air. It felt like the last moment before your ears pop after coming down from a height.

At the station he was met by the plant Manager, a ruddy-faced man who shook his hand warmly and smiled a lot. He was pleased to see the young man, he said, beaming. Very pleased indeed. They had heard glowing reports of the young man down the wire. They would do whatever they could to assist such an eminent fellow.

When the young man replied he felt the föhn breeze tug at his words like a kite and realised then why this place was so quiet. He breathed the air deeply, like drinking water, and savoured it.

THE WORKS

He had been given a spruce panelled room in a two-storey yellow brick building which was shaped like the prow of a boat, dividing the wide main street and the föhn breeze like a fin. It was the tallest building in town.

He had an office at the works, also. There the window looked out over the processing floor and afforded a good view of the comings and goings.

"What would you like us to do first?" the Manager enquired after he had shown the young man the view from his new office.

The young man shook his head. He had already noticed that people here made much use of non-verbal communication, as if to conserve words in the breeze.

"Nothing," he said. "That is very important. Please do nothing differently until I'm ready. I need calibration."

The Manager nodded, seeing at once how sensible this was. "Just let us know, then," he said.

HANNY

And so, for several months, the young man studied and assessed and made measurements. The plant workers grew used to seeing him standing silently beside the pump gauges or noting how a flow valve was set. The inhabitants of the town would see him striding the length of Main Street on his way to the reed beds, or watching the wind tower on the Eastside embankment as it hummed.

The inhabitants of the town grew to like the quiet, solitary young man. They liked him because he was quiet and because he listened to them when he had asked a question in his odd, stilted way. He did not interrupt when they answered. He was not quick to judge.

Some thought the young man must have been sent there because he had made some minor transgression. The province of K____ was not a place one would ask to be sent, although to any native K____lander it was not a place one could ever ask to leave.

The townspeople had been told the young man's name, of course, but it did not come out right in the local dialect so instead they called him *Hanny* which means *quiet* in the sense of reserved. The young man did not mind this and he became used to it.

SILVERFISH

Early in his work the young man – *Hanny* – spent several weeks at the hot pools to the north of town where he watched and calculated the various flows. Often when he was there he would see off-shift men from the plants fishing in the lagoons. They would nod as they passed him with their rods, and when they returned with the local silverfish on a string.

After a year he asked one of the men to teach him how to fish. He recognised the simplicity in the arc of a cast and the vectors of the drift caused by wind or the slow pool current. He enjoyed the company of the other anglers, too, because mostly it was silent and contemplative.

After two years he met a girl called Alana who had long brown hair and a cheery smile. When they walked out together the locals would smile to see the two of them. They thought that this meant that *Hanny* would become one of them.

"I think you're becoming one of us," Alana told him one afternoon as they strolled towards the salt bins so *Hanny* could measure their levels. By now he had started to implement changes at the plant which required constant monitoring.

Hanny nodded and squeezed her hand, meaning he thought so, too.

"Are you content?" Alana asked. "We're not too provincial for you? You wouldn't like to return to the city?"

He shook his head. "The city is too loud for me," he said. "Out here you can be silent."

"You've discovered our secret," Alana said with a smile.

"I've discovered *many* things since I came here," he said, and she knew what he meant. It made her feel happy.

"What will you do when the work is complete?"

"I think Bart would like me to be Deputy Manager," *Hanny* said. "He has mentioned that he could use help."

Alana smiled again and tugged at his arm so that he bent down where she could kiss his cheek. This meant "Good." When they reached the salt bins she helped him to measure.

REMAINING

Every month *Hanny* was required to file a report on his work and to list exact details and calibrations, describing exactly what changes had been made. He would walk out to the wire office and spend the morning reading his report aloud to the telegraphist who tapped the key in staccato.

On the third anniversary of his arrival *Hanny* filed a report stating that all the adaptations at the plant were complete. It now remained to monitor the change in output and productivity.

To the report he also appended a short letter to the man in gabardine and silk informing him of his intention to remain in K_____ once his present task was complete, perhaps as Deputy Manager of the plant. He received no reply to the letter but several months later a stranger alighted from the train.

THE STRANGER

The stranger clearly did not find the föhn breeze to his liking. Nor did he seem comfortable in the silence. He seemed annoyed that it would be thirteen days until the next train.

In town the stranger asked for *Hanny* by his old name and seemed perplexed when no-one recognised it. It took several attempts before someone realised that the stranger must be enquiring about *Hanny*. They had all quite forgotten that *Hanny* had not been there for ever.

Following directions the stranger found *Hanny* at the hot pools. He was not fishing because he was at a stage of his work where there was little time for recreation. Also, his marriage to Alana was only a few days away so it was important to have things in order.

When the stranger found him, *Hanny* was calculating the depth of a pool from a short platform built out into the water from the bank. He paused in his workings to return to the bank where the stranger stood. He required no introduction because his clothes spoke for him.

For a few moments the stranger spoke cordially to *Hanny*, passing comment on the train journey and his impressions of the town. After this he told *Hanny* about the world beyond K_____.

"The Errid has become more frequent," he said.

Hanny pursed his lips a little, meaning "Is that so?"

"There are signs of encroachment in the south. People are afraid. There has been unrest in the cities. There have been deaths."

Hanny made a smoothing gesture with his left hand, an expression of sympathy and concern.

"Doesn't that mean anything to you?" the stranger said, more forcefully now, voice rising against the föhn. "Have you nothing to say?"

Realising that the stranger knew nothing of the conservation of words in the föhn breeze *Hanny* said: "I understand."

"Then you must also understand that it is even more imperative that you should complete your work here and return."

Hanny was silent for a time. Finally he said: "I feel my place is here."

"You are wrong. God damn this wind."

The stranger turned his back on it.

"I am—" He hesitated for a moment. "I am empowered to tell you that on the basis of your reports down the wire your work has been elevated to the very highest priority. It is no longer a matter of what you can achieve here. The Leader has seen the possibilities, the potential in what you are doing. You are an asset in the struggle and no man can ask for more."

"I would ask for less," *Hanny* said quietly. "Much less."

"What? I can't hear you. God damn this wind."

Hanny said nothing, but he made the gesture for "That is an end of it: I have nothing to say."

He returned to the end of the platform over the turquoise silt of the pond and started to take another measurement as the silverfish darted curiously round the pilings.

DO NOT DOUBT IT

But as the afternoon wore on *Hanny* realised that, despite his gesture, this would not be the end of it. So, after work, he sought out the stranger at his lodgings.

He had hoped that he might convince the man to reconsider, but it was immediately clear that the stranger was resolute.

"When this project is complete you must return," he said. "You are required."

Hanny shook his head although there was no föhn wind inside.

"We are all part of the struggle," the stranger pressed. "We have no choice. Besides, you do not belong here. You have nothing in common with these yokels."

"That is not true," *Hanny* said. "I am one of them. I am soon to be married."

"Let me tell you something," the stranger said. "It's abundantly clear. This God damned wind has turned your senses. Why would you squander your talents here amongst these dumb bunnies? Where is your sense of duty? Where is your humanity? If you could see what the Errid has done and continues to do..."

"I am sorry for that," *Hanny* said. "But I will not leave."

He stood up and made for the door.

"Things can be done," the stranger said. "Do not doubt that. Never doubt it. It is why they sent me and not the man in gabardine and silk."

Hanny stopped in his tracks. He did not doubt this was true and in a moment he made up his mind.

He turned and strode back to the stranger, then he leaned down and spoke the stranger's numbers softly into his ear.

The stranger said nothing. He was perfectly still and he did not move or speak again when *Hanny* left the room, latching the door quietly behind him.

COLLODION

On the day of the wedding they undressed together and stood smiling for the collodion to be made. Many of the townspeople were there and they were happy to be part of this celebration. Ribbons twisted gaily in the breeze and there was cheerful, silent applause.

Afterwards Alana was taken away by the women – who were full of smiles and sly looks – to her grandmother's hut where the smell of baking was warm. *Hanny* was drawn by Bart's bear-like arm to the saloon where the men waited with thick glasses of thick plain beer to toast him in silence and sing.

In the evening the two wedding parties were brought together again and the ceremony was completed as it should be, with the bride and the groom bound by a single ribbon. Finally they were allowed to depart, leaving the others to continue the celebration and make merry.

As they walked up the quiet main street Alana held *Hanny*'s hand, which meant "You are one of us."

Hanny rubbed her thumb, which meant "I am complete."

STOLEN

Only the station master saw the stranger depart on the thirteenth day train. Since last speaking with *Hanny* he had remained in his room and taken his meals there. The station master reported that when he boarded the train the stranger had a ten-day beard and looked as if he had slept badly.

Later that day Alana was found by the small stand of wind-bent trees on the knoll. She seemed to be asleep but she was not. The town doctor said it was entirely probable that she had suffered a congenital weakness of the heart which no-one could have detected.

ALONE

Once the funeral had been completed, and as the white smoke from the pyre was born out across the plain by the föhn breeze, *Hanny* walked out to the hot pools. He began work with a renewed vigour and in silence. However, the föhn steals only words and not thought. Nor calculations.

GOODBYE

Four years after his arrival in K_____ *Hanny* received instructions to return to the city. He did not argue this time. He was given a parcel of dried silverfish by Alana's family who were sad to see him go. Several came to the rail station to say farewell.

On the platform Bart shook his hand silently which meant "goodbye."

Hanny boarded the train alone.

NEXT

On his return to the city the man who was no longer *Hanny* was met at the rail station by the man in gabardine and silk. He was told that the calculations and formulae he had produced while he was in K_____ had also been applied to several other plants and works. The results of this had already been felt. There had been a marked drop in the power of Errid and as a consequence the calculations would now be applied even more widely.

In his absence the man who was no longer *Hanny* had also been given a title: *Tær Desenr*. This was a mark of the regard in which he was now held. In a few days he would meet the Leader himself and then he would learn what was required of him next.

Tær Desenr said nothing, for the habits of the föhn were still deeply embedded within him. Slowly, however, he grew accustomed to the use of speech without gestures once again, although when he did speak he returned to his odd, stilted manner. When he was alone the föhn silence was more natural.

THE TALL DARK MEN

While he waited to be summoned to meet the Leader, *Tær Desenr* had little to occupy or interest him. At night he stood on the balcony of his high apartment in the hope of catching a breeze. But the air of the city was unmoving and foetid and sometimes *Tær Desenr* felt he was drowning.

Sometimes, when he could bear it no longer, *Tær Desenr* walked the streets, although he knew he was never alone on these walks. The tall dark men did not try to conceal their presence, only their faces beneath the brims of their hats. It was not hard for *Tær Desenr* to formulate a conclusion about what this must mean.

YOU KILLED ALANA

One night *Tær Desenr* turned a corner beneath a brick arch which still held the day's heat in its fabric. From a niche beneath the archway a figure moved out to confront him.

The man was dishevelled with many months of beard, but *Tær Desenr* recognised him almost at once as the stranger who had come to see him in the province of K____. In his hand the stranger held a knife. Out of instinct *Tær Desenr* made the föhn gesture which means *what* or *where* or *how*.

The stranger did not seem to understand, or perhaps did not care.

"Take back the numbers."

Tær Desenr shook his head.

"Unless you take back those numbers I am going to kill you," the stranger said. His eyes were white-yellow and wide in the darkness.

Tær Desenr said slowly: "You killed Alana."

The stranger did not deny it. "I had orders," he said. "You would not listen. Take back the numbers!"

Tær Desenr shook his head. "I cannot. They are your numbers."

As the stranger lunged forwards *Tær Desenr* did not move to stop him. He awaited the plunge of the knife. But before he could feel it the tall dark men were there.

The struggle was brief. The knife fell to the floor, as well as a hat. The knife skittered and came to rest by *Tær Desenr*'s shoe.

While the stranger was subdued and removed *Tær Desenr* picked up the knife from where it had fallen. He knew what he must do now.

Ð

A reception was held for the noted and loyal. There were many men in formal attire and women like birds. Music played softly, the halls and marble stairs echoed with conversation and soft laughter.

After a time, in which he spoke to no-one but watched and counted from aside, *Tær Desenr* was led away from the others and guided to a library where he was left alone with the Leader.

"*Tær Desenr*, *Tær Desenr*," the Leader said warmly as he clasped his hand.

The servants and underlings left them now and they were alone. The Leader stood beside a marble fireplace as tall as a man. In the grate a wood fire burned, snapping occasionally as the Leader spoke.

Wordlessly *Tær Desenr* took the stranger's knife from his pocket. The Leader saw this but did not break from what he was saying.

"Let there be an understanding between us," he said. "An understanding that between us there can be no divide. Between us there is nothing we cannot achieve."

Tær Desenr took a step forward but still the Leader did not break from what he was saying. He did not look at the knife. His words became intimate and intent, like the music of thought. His words were like water, finding the cracks and crevices and spaces within *Tær Desenr* – for the Leader was to words what *Tær Desenr* was to numbers.

A log shifted in the fire and sent up a flurry of sparks. Still the Leader spoke, gently and comforting, and *Tær Desenr* thought of the huts and the pencils and apples. He thought of the silverfish and Alana and the province of K____ and knew these things could not be regained.

What else could he do? What else had he left? Only calculations.

He placed the knife on the mantel and studied the fire as the Leader spoke on.

OUTSIDE

When *Tær Desenr* emerged from the library some time later the man in gabardine and silk was waiting for him. He placed a hand on the other man's arm, as if in condolence.

"Come," he said. "A place has been prepared for you."

THE COUNT

And so a number of years passed during which *Tær Desenr* applied himself to the problems he was given. At first he would meet with his petitioners in person and listen quietly as they explained the nature of their particular problem. Soon, however, it became apparent that this took too much time, and instead *Tær Desenr* employed clerks and forms to catalogue and sift and extract the requests which he then considered alone.

If it was required, agents would be sent to gather more information. Sometimes this would take months. Sometimes – not often – there would be reports that an agent had died and another would have to be sent in their place. Sometimes a problem was solved very quickly.

Whether a problem took seconds or months *Tær Desenr* worked tirelessly at his task. Always alone.

Over time he developed his raw data into complex algorithms. He drew these calculations into blueprints and designs; into plans and long lists of specifications which would fill a book – would fill volumes – and did.

Over time these individual projects began to overlap – as *Tær Desenr* had anticipated they would – and at this point he reported to the Leader that it was now impossible to view anything in isolation. The parts had become so large and complex that they could only be seen as parts of a whole, and this construct was so large in its conception, so interconnected and pervasive of all things, that the only simple thing about it was its name: The Count.

FOR A CHANGE

Every so often, without notice, the tall dark men in hats would bring a car and take *Tær Desenr* to see the Leader. The two of them would discuss different matters beside a wood fire and afterwards the man in gabardine and silk would accompany *Tær Desenr* back to his work.

However, one day after such a meeting, the man in gabardine paused as they were about to enter the car. He said: "Shall we walk for a change? It's a pleasant afternoon. The fresh air might agree with us."

When *Tær Desenr* agreed that it might the man in gabardine dismissed the car and its tall dark driver and together they strolled companionably through the streets and boulevards. *Tær Desenr* walked a little more slowly than he might otherwise have done because the man in gabardine and silk was not as sprightly as he had once been.

When they had walked for several minutes they reached the end of the boulevard and paused at the kerb. *Tær Desenr* noticed a line of people waiting to approach a booth which stood at the corner of the street.

"What are they waiting for?" he asked the man in gabardine and silk.

"Their fortunes."

"I don't understand."

"A token is purchased or given as a gift," the man in gabardine explained. "It is inserted in the machine and a handle is gripped, then the fortune teller produces a reading."

"That is curious."

"Would you like to try? "

Tær Desenr thought for a moment, then nodded and the two of them joined the end of the line. The man in gabardine and silk gave *Tær Desenr* three tokens.

When they reached the machine a few minutes later the man in gabardine and silk showed *Tær Desenr* where to insert a token and how to grasp the heavy brass lever just right. *Tær Desenr* cranked it forward with just the right pressure, like punching a hole.

Behind the glass Madam Sryer's mannequin face bowed in concentration and the dummy hand moved its dry pen mechanically back and forth in a simulation of writing. It lasted a few seconds and then the movement ceased. Below the glass booth, from within, there was a thud and a small card was ejected into a slot. In one jerky movement Madam Scryer snapped back to her starting position and was still.

Tær Desenr retrieved the card from the slot and they moved away from the machine to let the next person in line take their turn.

The card was a dusty yellow.

"*A pleasant memory of a happy incident in your life will be brought back to you by a meeting with an old friend. A happy and prosperous period is ahead of you. Problems which have been troubling you of late will be solved in the most simple manner and you will be left wondering what all the worry was about. The most pleasant part of your life lies before you.*"

Tær Desenr looked from the card to his companion.

"It is simply a random choice of a pre-produced card."

"Exactly that," the man in gabardine nodded. "It is an interpretation of one of your calculations."

"That is curious," *Tær Desenr* said. "I would like to watch for a while."

"Of course," the man in gabardine said. "But if you will excuse me: my legs are not as good as they were."

"Of course."

AGAIN

When the man in gabardine and silk had departed *Tær Desenr* moved closer to the fortune machine, the better to observe its mechanics. Fourteen people approached it and pulled the heavy lever to receive their card.

After a while *Tær Desenr* joined the end of the line once again and after a short wait he inserted his second token before pulling the lever. When he retrieved the cherry red card he moved away. Beneath his fingers he could feel the deeply impressed print of the card but he did not read it until he stood beside an awning at the corner of the block.

"A pleasant memory of a happy incident in your life will be brought back to you by a meeting with an old friend..."

He compared the card to the one from his first token. Apart from the colour it was exactly the same.

"Is it good?"

Surprised by the voice, *Tær Desenr* turned to see a young woman. She, too, had a fortune card in her hand: blue.

JULIA

"I like Madam Scryer the best," the young woman went on. "She always seems to know just what I'm thinking."

She was quite plain, but there was a directness in her eyes which matched the sway of the light summer dress she was wearing.

"My name is Julia," she told him and held out her hand. When he held it he knew her plainness was merely an illusion. He knew that when she was naked and rapt in love making he would find her as beautiful as anyone could ever be, with small breasts and a dense bush like a jungle.

"It's nice to meet you," he said.

"And you."

"May I ask – your card, what does it say?"

Julia held up the green fortune card in her hand. "It says: '*Someone is impatiently waiting to see you. You know who I mean.*'"

"Do you?" he asked.

"I think so," she said with a smile.

"That's good then."

"I think so," she said.

Then the horns of the Errid warning sounded. On the damp street there was a momentary pause as people stopped to look up anxiously at the grey sky before quickening their steps towards shelter.

Tær Desenr did not move but he, too, peered upwards, as if waiting to see Errid in the rain-wet sky.

"We should go to a shelter," Julia told him, looping her arm through his.

Tær Desenr shook his head. "It's not necessary," he said.

Julia looked at him inquisitively but not afraid. She did not let go of his arm. "I have a room across the street, that way," she said. "We could go there. It is only temporary. Tomorrow I'm leaving for the province of K_____."

"Of course."

DO YOU REMEMBER?

When they made love he found her as beautiful as anyone could ever be.

Afterwards, as they lay on the eiderdown which had been placed in a cube of sunlight on the wooden floor, Julia said: "Do you remember the apple bowling?"

"Yes."

"It was dandy, wasn't it?" she asked, shifting a little.

"Yes."

He moved his hand to cup her small breast. His thumb rubbed her nipple absently, like an acorn. He thought of what this would mean in the föhn breeze.

IN THE FAR LANDS

THE DAY OF THE TEA DANCE

In the morning the house was filled with different smells – roasting meat and bread and syrup – and I wondered if the Siisters had worked all night. It seemed to me that they might have.

As soon as I had eaten breakfast Simone gave me a list of things to do in preparation for the Tea Dance that afternoon. It was a long list and very detailed but I didn't mind because I knew that the success of the Tea Dance meant a lot to them both. I was glad to have something to concentrate on.

Among the things I had to do were arranging the tables; setting up the gramophone; hanging ribbons from Simian fisher's nets; counting the forks and sweeping the canvas dancing square. Leaves had blown in on the tightly stretched canvas.

While I did all these things and many others Elaine and Simone passed back and forth from the kitchen to the garden carrying all the cakes and pastries and meats and sandwiches and cordials they had prepared. They placed them on two long tables under the nets. At a third, smaller, table they set out fine china cups and saucers next to the tea urn so that the guests would be able to re-fill their cups as many times as they liked.

My final job was to tie open the gate at the top of the granite steps. Elaine gave me a length of ribbon to do that. "I don't want that fucking gate biting anyone today," she said. "The people who come here are our guests and they don't want to be bitten by a lousy goddamn gate."

I could see she had a point so I tied the gate firmly, just to let it know.

When I returned to the Tea Room after I'd tied the gate I saw that Elaine and Simone had changed from their everyday clothes and now wore velvet skirts which ended above their neatly laced boots. Elaine's skirt was green and Simone's was black. They also wore blouses which were trimmed with lace and left their shoulders bare. Elaine's red hair and Simone's yellow hair could swish back and forth across naked skin. It swished as they moved to stand in the centre of the Flying Horse Tea Room and wait for their guests.

"So, we are ready," Simone said with some satisfaction.

"Ready as we'll ever be," Elaine said. "Who do you suppose will arrive first?"

I thought it was strange that they couldn't guess who would arrive first because they always dreamed of Arrivals.

AN AWKWARD BEGINNING

After an hour the Siisters began to grow irritable. Simone in particular. They hadn't moved from the centre of the Tea Room and no-one had arrived.

"They said they were coming, so where are they?" Simone said. "How come they're keeping us waiting like this?"

"I can't tell," Elaine said. "Maybe they have a different idea of when a Tea Dance should start."

"It isn't good enough," Simone said. Elaine and I could both tell she was losing her patience.

"Perhaps Issy would go up to the gate and see if she can see any of the guests," Elaine suggested.

"Of course," I said. "I'll go now."

When I reached the top of the granite steps I was pleased to see that the gate was still tied back and behaving itself. I stepped out through it and looked along the street.

A few yards away on the opposite side of the street I saw Charlie, Mr Meyer, standing with Nancé and Dot. The other guests were standing near them, all talking amongst themselves except for those who didn't feel comfortable with small talk and preferred to remain quiet.

There were some other people who were not guests there, also. They had come to see why the guests were standing together looking across the road at the Flying Horse Tea Room as if the were waiting for something to happen. They had wondered what the gathering was in aid of.

I crossed the road towards the guests and when Charlie saw me coming he stepped forward.

"Good afternoon, Issy," Charlie said. "Are we expected yet or should be we continue to wait here a while longer?"

"The Siisters expected you all an hour ago," I told him. "The gate is tied back and everything's ready."

"Ah," Charlie said then. "Ah. I see. There seems to have been a misunderstanding. Perhaps we had better come now, then."

"I think Elaine and Simone would appreciate that," I said and I led the way back across the road towards the Tea Room.

THE GUESTS ARRIVE

The guests followed me one by one down the granite steps to the Tea Room. Charlie, Mr Meyer, was first behind me.

"I hope you haven't forgotten that we would like to speak with you at the Hall tomorrow, Issy," he said.

"I haven't forgotten," I said.

"Good."

The guests followed me in through the door of the Tea Room and I led them right up to the place where Elaine and Simone were waiting to welcome them.

"Dear Elaine. Dear Simone," Charlie said with a small bow. "Thank you for inviting us all to this occasion. We very much appreciate it."

Simone and Elaine both smiled. They were no longer irritable.

"We are very pleased to see you, Charlie," one of them said. It might have been Simone.

Charlie looked round at the Tea Room which was now almost bare of furniture. "Is the Tea Dance going to be in here?" he asked.

"No, no," Elaine said. "We wanted to do something very different. Issy, would you like to show our guest through to the garden? We will wait here to welcome the others."

"Of course," I said, quite formally. "This way please, Mr Meyer."

At that Charlie nodded and I led him to the tall door at the back of the tea room and up the short flight of mossy steps to the garden.

"My," he said when he got to the top of the steps and saw what the Siisters had been preparing. "I wasn't expecting this."

THE START OF THE TEA DANCE

The Siisters had timed it just right, despite the delay at the beginning. The afternoon sun was in just the right place and there was just enough breeze to move the branches of the garden trees gently. When they moved they let in small patches of sunlight which reflected and refracted from the mirrors and sequins in Simian fisher's nets. It looked as if the nets were winking.

When everyone had come through from the Tea Room and taken a seat Simone made a short speech of welcome. While she did this I noticed that two people who had said they would come had not come, at least not yet. One was Patrice, the other was Simian fisher.

I also noticed that amongst the guests who had been invited there were several who had not. These were people who had been standing with the guests as they waited in the street. Clearly they had decided to come along to the Tea Room and see what all the fuss was about. I wondered if Simone would say anything about this in her short speech of welcome, but she did not. Simone was nothing if not a considerate hostess.

After the speech Elaine started the gramophone and then she and Simone waltzed together on the burgundy canvas dancing floor. They did this so that the guests – invited or not – would not feel self-conscious about starting to dance. It seemed to do the trick. Pretty soon lots of people were dancing: more than those who were not.

Charlie danced with Nancé; Martin danced with Dot; Wendell danced with someone who had not been invited and I danced with Per si-Lversum. Later we changed partners. Later still we sat down to rest and drink tea and eat the food the Siisters had prepared, and others who had previously been sitting and drinking and eating got up to take our places.

When Elaine and Simone finished dancing with each other and others they stood beside the tea urn and smiled as they watched the way the Tea Dance was progressing. They seemed pleased that in spite of an awkward beginning, things had turned out so well.

FIVE THINGS IN ORDER

I think I should say that several hours passed and the Tea Dance continued with no sign of what was to come. Several things happened in that time and I will tell them in order.

The first thing was that Per si-Lversum talked to Elaine about the nets. He asked if Simian fisher had been invited to the Tea Dance. Elaine said that he had.

"So where is he?" asked Per.

"We're not sure," Elaine said. "But we're sure that he's late."

The second thing that happened was that after I had been dancing and resting and dancing some more I sat down at a table where Nancé was eating mutton stew with a fork. She was concentrating on this but when I sat down she smiled at me and said, "Hello, Issy."

I noticed her dress then. It was new and quite short. I saw that the bodice was made from the purple and green embroidery in the shape of house martins which she had shown me when I took her the invitation to the Tea Dance.

"That's a nice dress," I told her.

"Thank you," she said. "Do you recognise the embroidery?"

I told her I did. I also said that I could see the wrong stitch. It was what drew my eye most.

"I told you," she said. "It always happens once you know where it is. I just hope no-one else notices."

I said that I didn't think they would.

After I had talked to Nancé for a time and she had finished her stew we noticed that Simone had lit candles in jam jars.

This is the third thing that happened, in order. We hadn't realised until then that the afternoon had become evening. The candle light made new and different reflections in Simian fisher's nets.

The guests were dancing less energetically now and because they had more time to notice these things several of them commented on the difference made by the candles. Some also wondered how long the Tea Dance would continue but no-one seemed to mind that they didn't know. This was an unprecedented event and they wanted to make the most of it.

The fourth thing that happened was that I spoke to Martin and then to Dot by the tea urn. Dot had put her hair up in an intricate braid with several enamel pins to hold it in place. She looked like a statue.

"We'd like to thank you for talking to Patrice the other day," Martin said. "We think it helped. He has started to speak again, although it's mostly in numbers."

I didn't think I would tell them that I hadn't liked Patrice's numbers. Instead I said: "I'm glad about that."

"We wished he could have come with us to this Tea Dance," Dot told me. "But he wanted to stay at Wendell's Place. We don't know why."

"Perhaps he had things to count," I said.

"Perhaps so," Martin agreed.

The fifth thing that happened was that Simian fisher arrived. When he arrived he wasn't alone.

LATE ARRIVALS

"Hello, girls," Simian fisher said when he came into the garden. "Sorry we're late. Did we miss anything important?"

Simian was wearing his turned down sea boots and a wool hat on his head. He smelled strongly of fish, laced through with apple cider. The three other men who had come in behind him smelled the same way. They stood in a pretty straight line but they swayed in their boots. They were looking at the cakes and the food on the tables. They looked hungry enough for six.

"I knew you wouldn't mind me bringing a few of the boys along," Simian fisher went on. "Thought maybe you could all use a little pep in the proceedings about now, if you know what I mean."

Elaine looked at Simone. They were standing beside the tea urn.

"We know what you mean, Simian," Simone said. "But we're not sure we agree."

That was when Livia Stevens stood up. She said: "I don't believe you and your friends were invited to this Tea Dance, Simian."

She had quite forgotten that she hadn't been invited either. She had come in with Charlie and the others from across the road to see what was going on, but that was many hours ago now. After all the dancing and tea drinking it seemed like everyone who was there was supposed to be there. It seemed like it was those who had come late – invited or not – who were the intruders.

"I don't give a shit what you believe, Livvy," Simian said then. "I got *my* invite. How about you?"

When Simian said this Livia Stevens remembered that she hadn't had an invitation and she went to sit down again.

"You *were* invited, Simian," Elaine said in the way you might speak to a child. "We asked you to come. But there are limits. Your invitation did not say '*and guests*'."

We all knew she was talking about Simian's friends standing behind him in a pretty straight line, eyeing the cakes.

"You only asked me 'cause you had needs," Simian said. "For my nets, and for other things we won't go into here."

"Be that as it may," Simone said. "We won't go into it here. You're welcome to our Tea Dance, Simian, and your friends may stay, too. It's lucky for you that we have plenty of tea."

So saying she turned to the tea urn and started to fill the cups which Elaine passed her.

"Looks like we're in, boys," Simian said to his friends. "Let's drink tea for a change."

TEA

To help out with the sudden rush at the tea urn I cut lemon for the Siisters and passed out plates for the cake. I will say this for Simian's friends, they all said "Thank you, Issy". They drank their tea and took cake very appreciatively, as if it was a long time since they had done anything like this.

As the boys stood in a line and ate cake there was a short moment of silence until Charlie, Mr Meyer, wound up the gramophone again. Once there was music to fill the silence the other guests started to talk again. One or two decided to dance, now that they'd rested. Others came across to Simian and his friends to strike up conversations with people who hadn't been at the Tea Dance from the start and so could be relied upon to have a different perspective.

After a few more minutes it felt like there had never been an interlude at all and the hole it had made was closed like tea going into a cup.

THERE WILL BE TROUBLE

"There will be trouble, Issy," Per si-Lversum told me. "I'm pretty sure of it now and I'm too old for that. I don't think I'll stay any longer. I don't like the look of it."

As he said it he was watching one of the men who had come to the Tea Dance with Simian fisher. The man was talking to Nancé and as he did so he was looking at the embroidery on her bodice. He reached out a hand to stroke it and a moment later he pulled back the hand sharply. I saw the red glistening of blood on his finger.

"Shit!" he said loudly. And then more regretfully he said, "I wished I hadn't done that."

I knew he had found the wrong stitch.

Per si-Lversum had watched this happen, too. He put a hand on my shoulder. "If you feel like a cup of joe later I'll be brewing some," he said. "Say goodbye to the Siisters for me, okay?"

I told him I would and with that he went home.

When they saw that Per was leaving several other people thought they would leave too. They included Wendell and Martin and Dot. They had a long way to walk home and it was already dark so they said they would make a start now.

"Goodbye," Simone and Elaine said. "Thank you for coming to the Tea Dance. It was wonderful to see you."

"I hope you folks aren't leaving on account of us," Simian fisher said when he saw them heading towards the exit. He said it like it was an accusation.

"No, of course not," Martin said.

"You should've brought that boy of yours here and kept an eye on him," Simian went on as if Martin hadn't spoken. "'Stead of letting him come down to the quay bothering us with his numbers."

When he said this Dot turned to look at him, her eyes wide in a question. Her face was suddenly pale.

"The quay?" she said. "No, it couldn't have been Patrice. We left him at home at Wendell's Place."

"That might be where you left him, missis," Simian said. "But it ain't where he stayed. He's been down on the quay all afternoon. Ask Walt and Tertius here, you don't believe me. Ask French. He'll tell you."

"I don't understand," Wendell said. He looked concerned now and he cast a worried glance towards Charlie, Mr Meyer.

"What's not to understand?" Simian said. He sounded more angry now as if he didn't like it that people would not take his word. "The. God. Damn. Kid. Was. On. The. Quay. Get me?"

When he'd said it he reached up a hand and pulled a length of rope out of the net above his head.

The whole garden was quiet now. No-one else spoke. The gramophone played a foxtrot but no-one paid it any attention. Instead they were listening to Simian fisher.

"It's okay for you," Simian went on, looking at Martin. "You only just come here. For you everything here's still hunky and dory. But some of us who've been here for longer, we know different now, thanks to that kid."

FINE AND DANDY

"Some of us don't think we'll ever be Gone," Simian fisher said next. "And you know what? Some of us don't think we should ever have come here the first place. We are doubting the idea of it. Right now. That's when we're doubting it."

Simian was twisting and untwisting the rope as he said this. Then he smacked it against the side of his boot.

"God-dammit," he said with the smack. "It's fine and dandy for the likes of you, but some of us are lost. And some of us don't see the end of it. That's how we feel."

For a moment there was silence then the Siisters stepped forward to the centre of the canvas dancing floor.

"We want you to leave now," the Siisters said together and they hitched up their skirts so the men knew they meant business. "We want you to leave or we won't be responsible."

"Leave? We ain't leaving," the man called Tertius said. "We only just got here. Look at them cakes."

"I came here to dance," the man called French said. He was the one who had pricked his finger of Nancé's wrong stitch. Despite this he pulled her towards him and put his arm round her waist, ready to dance.

"Call this a Tea Dance," Simian said. "Let's have some pep."

Ignoring the Siisters he strode over to the gramophone and searched through the records until he found a polka.

"Now this is the sort of music we really need," he said. "You can have too much of that waltzing stuff."

"Good night One and All," Martin said as he ushered Dot and Wendell to the door. "Thank you for a splendid event."

THE END OF THE TEA DANCE

In the centre of the dancing square the Siisters stood motionless. Their skirts were still hitched to show they meant business but Simian fisher and his friends didn't seem to care. When the polka began to play the man called French started to whirl Nancé around the dance floor and I saw a smile creep slowly on to her face.

"We think you should go to your room now, Issy," the Siisters said when they moved off the dance floor out of French's way. "It's late and this is the end of the Tea Dance. Whatever happens next will not be the Tea Dance. We don't know what it will be but we don't think it will involve very much tea."

"Are you sure?" I asked her. "There are still lots of guests, even if some are uninvited. Would you like me to help you turn this into some other kind of party?"

"You're very kind, Issy," Elaine told me. "But I think what we've said is for the best. Please let us guide you in this."

I was disappointed but I tried not to show it. I knew the Siisters.

TOO MANY STEPS

I must have slept for a time. When I woke it was still middle-of-the-night-dark. Through the open window I could hear sounds from outside and below. They were the sounds of shouts and things being broken and also some singing. The sounds rang out and came upwards from the otherwise stillness of the Town.

When I went to the window I could see that French had carried the gramophone into the street and set it up on the cobbles to play polkas. The sounds drifted upwards and I saw many more people than those who had been invited to the Tea Dance. They had gathered themselves together and they were having their own Tea Dance, or perhaps it was simply an extension of the Siisters' soirée. I did not think so, though, because I could not see the Siisters and I felt they would be there if this was anything to do with them.

In the street below the candles and lanterns and lamps seemed to ebb and flow like a tide. After I had watched for a while a great cheer went up as someone new was brought to join in. In the flickering light I could see that this person was Patrice.

Patrice walked strangely. I saw that his hands were behind his back, both of them. Simian fisher and Walt and Tertius and French lined up to speak to him but Patrice did not raise his head. He stood with his chin on his chest.

I remembered what Per had said when he said "There will be trouble" and I thought that he was correct. I could not see Per amongst the people below in the street.

I left the window and went to the door of my room only to find that it was locked. I did not have a key and I had not locked it. I wondered who had.

I stood by the door thinking what to do. I could hear voices from below, and footsteps. I heard voices on the landing, but after 76 steps already, the remaining stairs to my room must have been too many to deal with. After a while I heard the voices going away, downwards. I was glad that there were 89 steps to my room and went back to the window.

The street was empty now. When I looked to the left I could see the tail-end stragglers of the crowd as they all headed towards the Square. Their sound was a murmur, but as I turned to move away from the window I heard a much louder cheer go up from the Square. I knew that something had Happened but as I did not know what I went back to bed.

THE TEA ROOM IS CLOSED

In the morning my door was not locked and I wondered if I had been mistaken that it had ever been so.

The Siisters were not in the kitchen, nor in the Tea Room. When I looked in the Tea Room I saw that the floor was covered in broken cake and spilled liquids, some of them cordials, some not.

Outside in the garden several tablecloths had fish-oily foot prints on them although they were still on the tables. Many teacups were cracked or broken and Simian fisher's nets had been pulled down from the trees and piled in a heap on the canvas dancing square. I looked at all this for several moments and then I went back inside.

I went to the Siisters' room and knocked on the door but there was no reply. There was silence from beyond the wood. The Siisters might have been there or they might not, I didn't know. I went back down the steps to the Tea Room and started to sweep up the broken cakes and mop the spilled liquids.

After I'd done that for a while I remembered the gate. I went behind the counter and found out a piece of card on which to write a message. When I'd done that I climbed the granite steps to the gate and untied the ribbon which had stopped it from biting people. I let it swing closed, then I used the ribbon to hang up the message I had written. It said "*The Flying Horse Tea Room is temporarily closed. Thank you for your understanding, love Issy.*"

It was the first time the Flying Horse Tea Room had been closed during the day time since I could remember. It might have been the only time it had ever been closed.

I worked to clear up the mess in the Tea Room and the garden. I put the broken and damaged teacups and plates in a basket and fed the chickens with the cakes and pastries that had been broken and stomped on the floor. They didn't seem to mind that the food was squashed. It was all the same to them.

After I'd done this, and swept the floor, I remembered that today was the day I had said I would go and talk to Charlie, Mr Meyer at the Hall. Because I'd said that I would do this I thought I had better do so, even though there was still some clearing up to do at the Flying Horse Tea Room. I knew it would still be there when I got back so I thought I had better change my shoes.

DISAPPOINTED

The Siisters had still not come out of their room. When I passed their room on my way up the 89 steps to the top of the house I knocked on the door. After a few moments one of them said "Is that you, Issy?" It might have been Elaine.

"Yes, it's me, I said. "Are you coming out now?"

"We're too disappointed to come out," might-have-been-Elaine said.

"I understand that," I said.

"We're very, very disappointed," might-have-been-Elaine said. "It may take us several days to get over it. It may take us more. We can't tell yet. Is the Tea Room open?"

I told her it wasn't. I told her about the sign I'd put on the gate. After a moment she said: "I think that's for the best. We'll leave it to you, Issy. We're too disappointed to do more than that now."

I told her I was going to change my shoes before I went to see Charlie, Mr Meyer but all I heard was an understanding silence.

When I passed the Siisters' room on my way back down again with different shoes I saw that a note had been pushed under the door. It said: *Dear Issy we would like you to take tea with us this afternoon in the closed Flying Horse Tea Room. Your loving friends Elaine and Simone.*"

I found a pencil and wrote a reply on the back of the note. It said: *"I will be there. Love from Issy."*

SEEING CHARLIE

The first thing I noticed outside the Very Tall House was the gramophone in the middle of the street. The second thing I noticed was that the street was very quiet.

As I walked along the street to the Hall I also noticed that there was no-one else about. It was as quiet as a very early in the morning, except that it wasn't. I saw one of Elaine's favourite teacups alone on a gatepost.

When I arrived at the Hall the doors at the bottom of the steps were open. I went down the steps and inside. That was where I saw Charlie, Mr Meyer, sitting at a green baize table with a sheet of paper. He had a pen in his hand.

"Hello, Ithy," Charlie said as I came across the floor of the Hall towards him. "Thank you for coming."

Charlie's bottom lip was split on the left side. It was the colour of redcurrants. His top lip was split very close to the centre and it was swollen like a ripe grape. His left eye was the colour of a rotten banana except where it was as blue as a plum.

"It was no problem," I told him. "You don't look so good."

"I've had worth," he said. "But not lately. Thothe boyth play for keepth."

He put a delicate finger to the split on his lower lip as if to be sure it was still there.

"I don't know if you've heard what'th happened," he thaid then. "Thingth have changed thince lasth night."

"What sort of things," I asked.

"One of them ith Thimian fither," he thaid. "Another ith Walter boatman, and another ith Tertiuth Monday. They have left the ith-Landth."

"You mean they have Gone?" I asked.

Charlie shook his head. "I mean they have left. They were theen thith morning taking Thimian'th thmall yellow dinghy out through the harbour entranthe and thetting a thail."

"Perhapth they've jutht gone to an off-island," I said. Charlie's lisp was very infectious. "Maybe they jutht wanted to get away for a while."

"We don't think tho," Charlie said, shaking his head. "They thailed into the dithtanth and didn't change courthe. They took no netth with them. We think they have left the ith-Landth altogether. After everything that wath thaid and done latht night it theemth like the motht likely thenario."

I was shaken by this news. It wasn't something I had ever heard of before. I wasn't even sure it was a thing that was possible to do.

I asked Charlie if I might sit down for a moment and he got up and brought a folding chair to the other side of the table for me to sit on. As he did this I noticed that he had a very bad limp in his left foot.

OTHER THINGTH

"Have other things happened as well," I asked Charlie after I had been sitting on the folding chair for a moment.

"Other thingth *are* happening even ath we thpeak," Charlie told me. "I am writing my rethignation ath Meyer. Altho, thome people have told me that theveral men are building a raft on Trenarren beach tho that they can leave the ith-Landth like Thimian did. They are drinking ath they build the raft, tho there ith thome doubt about whether it will float when it'th finithhed, but if it doeth it theemth certain they will at leatht *try* to leave."

"But if people start leaving without going..." I said.

"Exactly," Charlie said. "But what can we do? Ath far ath I can thee there ith nothing we *can* do."

I shook my head. "Is it even possible?" I said. "My father always said not."

"It hath never been tried before," Charlie said. "It hath alwayth been an article of faith. But maybe our faith hath been mithplaced all thith time."

He looked down sadly at the sheet of paper he'd been writing on when I came in.

"I have enjoyed my time being Mr Meyer," he said. "It gave me a great deal of comfort. But after latht night I think I thould thtop. And becauthe of that it wouldn't be appropriate for me to talk of the matter I intended to talk to you about today. I will leave that to my thucthethor."

"Your thucthethor?" I asked. His lisp had become really quite bad.

"The one who repla— The *new* Mr Meyer."

"Ah," I said. "I see."

"How are the Thiithterth?" he asked.

"I'm not sure," I told him. "They are still in their room. I think they may be disappointed, though, knowing the Siisters."

"I quite underthtand," Charlie said. "Tho am I."

OPEN

When I left Charlie, not-Mr Meyer, in the Hall I walked back across the Square in the direction of the Very Tall House. I thought it was odd that I still saw no-one at all.

I did see that Nancé's door stood open on its many brass hinges, though. I wondered if it had been open when I passed on my way to the Hall and I hadn't noticed. Or had it been opened while I was with Charlie?

I decided that I couldn't remember, but I thought that I would go and see how Nancé had enjoyed the Tea Dance. I thought it would be easier to talk with someone who did not have a very bad lithp.

When I called at the door there was no reply, so I stepped over the threshold and went inside. Nancé was not in the parlour or in the kitchen. Her dress with house martins lay torn on the flagstones there, however.

This disturbed me. I knew it would disturb Nancé as well so I called out her name again and received no reply. I went to the foot of the stairs and called again. They were wooden stairs, very old: 11. I counted them as I waited for a reply but there was none. I waited a while longer, then I left the house through the open door.

I thought about my list of things that were disturbing:

Nancé's dress

Charlie's lisp and no longer being Mr Meyer

The gramophone on the cobbles

The rope with the noose hanging from a tree in the north corner of the Square.

The Flying Horse Tea Rooms being closed.

The silence.

Simian fisher (and others) leaving the is-Lands.

A raft being built.

I thought there were probably other things that I could add to the list as well but I wasn't quite able to bring them to mind. I was unsure what to do.

THE RAFT

I decided I would like to find someone to talk to.

I knew the Siisters did not want to talk and Charlie had said that it would be inappropriate for *him* to talk more, so I decided I would go to Trenarren beach where people were building a raft. Also I was curious to see the raft and ask what they hoped to achieve by building it.

So that is what I did.

Even while I walked to the beach I saw no one. I thought it might be that everyone was at the beach ahead of me. It would explain why there was no one to be seen in the Town or on the path to Trenarren beach, which is rocky and a steam runs beside it through peddarswrack plants which grow thick along its edge.

When I came to the beach – which was a wide cove of fine sand – I saw there were many people there, although not so many as would account for there being no-one in the Town or on the path.

There were two fires burning some distance apart. Between them people were assembling a raft just as Charlie had told me. The enterprise was a joint one, with many people bringing spars of wood and tying ropes and adjusting this thing or that thing or standing with hands on their hips to assess something.

It was a large raft, with a mast and a square sail and a spinnaker and a small cabin. I estimated that it might carry more than a dozen people.

After I had watched the raft building for a while I saw Marianna sitting on a solitary rock. She was watching the raft building also and I went over to her. She had bare feet in the sand beneath her dress which would have swished round her ankles if she had been walking.

"Hello Marianna," I said. "How are the trees?"

"Hello Issy," she said. Then: "Recalcitrant. But with rowans you have to expect that."

I sat down beside her. The sand was dry and warm in the morning sunlight. I watched the grains roll off my shoes, then I looked at the raft.

It seemed pretty much finished by now and many of those who had built it were standing back to look at their handiwork with their arms folded. It seemed that some of them had less enthusiasm for it now, as if they were not sure why they had spent their time on it and what might have possessed them to do so.

Then Al Klinglehofer stepped forward and stood on the raft. He turned to look at his fellow builders as if he suspected that their enthusiasm had waned.

"So what are we waiting for?" he said. "Written invitations? We all know what *they* mean. – So who's with me?"

It seemed that no-one had realised the question was aimed at them all because nobody moved.

"So who's with me?" Al Klinglehofer asked for a second time. "Who wants to get away from this godforsaken place? Let's go, people! Let's not have wasted our time here!"

Again there was silence, until finally Bill coining stood up from the sand. "Fuck it," he said. "Let's get this show on the road."

"Are they really going to leave?" I asked Marianna.

"It's what they've been saying," she said.

"Charlie, not-Mr Meyer, told me that Simian fisher, Walter boatman, and Tertius Monday have already sailed away," I said. "It's disturbing."

Marianna nodded. "I agree," she told me.

SEND US A POSTCARD

By now Al Klinglehofer and Bill coining had been joined by half a dozen others and they were making preparations to set sail. The raft was close to the edge of the sea, but not in it. The waves – which were small and lazy – did not quite reach the barrels at the front of the craft.

Those people who had not moved to get on to the raft and sail away were marshalled together to push the raft into the water. They pushed a lot and very hard but the raft did not move.

There were discussions then, between those people on the raft and those people pushing, and after the discussions all the people who had got on to the raft in preparation for sailing had to get off again and lend their weight to the pushing.

"Shall we help?" I asked Marianna. "It looks like they could use it."

"I'll watch," she said, as if somebody had to. "You go."

So I took off my shoes and went down the sand to the raft.

I helped the others and together we pushed the raft into the sea, although it wasn't as easy as it might sound. Then those who had got off the raft waded into the water and climbed aboard again, although some looked more tentative now that the raft was afloat and the adventure was imminent.

The raft had a list to one side and the water came higher than might have been intended but Al Klinglehofer directed the passengers to different positions and the raft became less lopsided. It rose and fell in the swell, just a little.

No-one had thought to make oars so the people on board the raft used their hands to paddle and slowly the raft moved away from shore. It moved very slowly because the waves – even though they were lazy – tried to push it back again. It was an equal fight and for a time it looked as if the waves might win.

Then Al and Bill coining unfurled the sail and it was enough to propel the raft forward through the lazy waves and when it seemed that they were finally making headway Al Klinglehofer came to stand on the stern and look back at the beach and wave.

"So long, suckers!" he shouted. "We'll send you a postcard!"

MISSING

Now that the raft was afloat and heading away, those people left on the beach stood around as if they had just woken up and were not entirely sure why they were not in their beds. I saw several people shrug as they turned away from the sea.

When I returned to Marianna I found she had been joined by Dot and Martin and Wendell who had not been there before and had not taken any part in the building or launching of the raft. They stood in a line in front of Marianna, their backs to the raft and the sea. When I sat down next to Marianna again I felt that they had been waiting for me.

"Good morning one and all," I said.

"Good morning, Issy," they said.

Then Martin said: "Patrice is missing."

THE LAST TIME WE SAW HIM

I thought about this because I could tell it was a serious matter to them. Not like a misplaced hair pin or cup.

"The last time we saw him was last afternoon at Wendell's place," Martin went on as I thought. "We left him there while we came to the Tea Dance."

I nodded because I remembered this being said.

"He musta left, though," Wendell told me. "Simian fisher and them said he'd been down at the harbour all afternoon telling his numbers."

I nodded again, because I remembered this being said also. I wondered why they were telling me things that I already knew and I waited for them to get to the point.

"The point is, something about this isn't right," Martin said and I saw Dot cast him a nervous look. "We are not sure how it could be that he was at Wendell's place and also at the harbour. Do you know?"

I nodded for a third time.

"Tell her about the rope," Dot said.

"There is a rope – a noose – on the branch of a tree in the Square," Martin told me. "It is disturbing."

"They're concerned," Wendell told me. "Kid's missing, you see a noose, what you gonna think?"

He raised his hands away from his sides a little way, then let them fall back so they slapped his legs. "I gotta get back to the sheep," he said, as if that put an end to it.

While Wendell left us I looked out to sea at the raft. I saw a splash and then someone was swimming back towards shore.

"What do you think, Issy?" Martin said, and I realised I had not heard the first part of what he had said because my attention had been elsewhere.

"About what?"

"Do you have any idea where Patrice might have gone?"

"I think I might," I said. "What would you like me to do?"

"We'd like you to find him, if you know where he might be," Martin said. "We're all disturbed by his absence. We think he should come back. We think—"

He broke off and looked at Dot who hesitated, then nodded.

"We think it would be best all round if he would come back," Martin told me. "There are things which need to be said. There are things which need to be addressed. Yes."

I could see that this was important so I nodded. "I will try then," I said. "I have an appointment with the Siisters, but after that I will see what I can do.

"Thank you, Issy," Dot said and she reached out a hand and touched mine. "Thank you."

MUTINY

I brushed the sand from my feet and put on my shoes. I stood up as the swimmer from the raft finally made shore and waded out of the water. It was Per, I saw then.

When he reached the dry land, dripping wet with his clothes sticking to him, he looked at the people who had waited to see him walk out of the water. Then someone asked what had happened.

"There was a mutiny," Per said. "I couldn't stand it. Good luck to them, that's all I can say. They'll send us a postcard."

We looked towards the raft. It was leaning precariously now as it rose and fell in the long, lazy swell. The breeze was pushing it sideways towards a sharp needle of rock.

As we watched we saw several figures on board move to the stern of the raft. There were splashes as some of them dived and others jumped into the sea before striking out towards the beach. One by one all the people on the raft abandoned ship until only Al Klinglehofer and Bill coining were left. I could tell it was them by their sweaters.

Al and Bill clung to the mast as the raft nuzzled the rock and then they, too, slipped into the water. Bill coining swam towards shore but Al set his course towards the horizon. He was swimming a long, lazy backstroke so perhaps he didn't know that he was heading in the wrong direction. Or maybe he didn't care. It is hard to endure a mutiny and a sinking in the same day.

CAKE AND CHICKENS

When I returned to the Very Tall House Near The Square from the beach I found that the Siisters were sitting at a table in the centre of the Tea Room. There was a pot of freshly made tea and three cups; ones which had not been damaged after the Tea Dance was over.

"Join us, Issy," the Siisters said in unison when I came into the Tea Room. "We have something to tell you."

I went to the table and sat down. Simone poured tea in the third cup and placed it in front of me as I shook the sand from my shoes.

"We have made a decision, Issy," Elaine told me. "We will not be re-opening the Flying Horse Tea Room."

"Are you still disappointed?" I asked her.

It was Simone who answered. "We think we have lost our way, Issy," she said. "The Tea Room was never meant to be our *raison d'être* but it was something that happened. We have thought about it while we've been in our room and we can see no sense in continuing with tea."

"What will you do, then?" I asked. It was hard to imagine the Siisters without seeing them behind the counter of cakes.

"We've thought about that, too," Elaine said. "But we don't have an answer. We're pretty sure something will occur to us but we cannot say what. Simone has some ideas."

"We wanted to tell you this, Issy, because we know that you loved the Tea Room. We know it was your reason for coming here from Fryst. Of course, you are welcome to stay in the room at the top of 89 or 77 steps for as long as you like. Or you may think that there is no reason to stay and climb so many steps to the room any more. We'll leave it to you."

"Thank you," I said. "I appreciate that."

We talked a little more as we sat at the table and then I said I would go up to my room for a while. As I stood up to do this Simone said: "Oh, I meant to ask you. Have you been feeding cake to the chickens?"

I said that I had.

"Ah," she said. "That   explains it. We wondered."

IN MY ROOM

In my room I thought about a lot of things. I could have made a list of the things I thought about. I wondered if that would help.

As I thought about things I wove some braids. I find that is helpful when I have many and different things to think about. I have sometimes wondered if the braids might become Works, or parts of Works, but it is too soon to say. It was another thing I thought about, but not for long as it was not so important right then.

By the time I had thought most of my thoughts it had grown dark outside and I thought it was too late to think about going to find Patrice. I thought I knew where I should go but I thought it was best not to go now. I thought I would wait until morning.

Outside, through the open window, I heard the sound of a very slow tarantella playing on the gramophone which was still on the cobbles of the street.

I stood up to look through the folded back windows. It was just possible to make out a figure, dancing with an imaginary partner. I thought the figure might be Nancé, but I couldn't be sure. She moved very slowly and sadly to the tarantella waltz and I hoped that it was Nancé. I had had worrying thoughts about what might have become of her since I found her torn dress on the floor. She was alone, even when I went to bed.

IN MY DREAMS

I was surprised to see my father standing on the cobbles of the quay next to a nicely rusted capstan with an oily rope wrapped around it. I was surprised because I had thought my father wouldn't be part of this story again.

"Hello, Issy," he said when he saw me. "I hadn't thought I would see you here."

"Neither did I," I said. "I thought you had Gone."

When I started to cry he put his arm round me. "You'll see me again," he said.

I shook my head, wordlessly.

"Of course," he said. "After all, you didn't expect me to be here now, did you? So who knows when else I will be there when you don't expect it? Things have a way of happening."

I was still too upset to speak because I knew that there was nothing I could say that would change things.

IN THE HARBOUR

We stood together on the quay and my father kept his arm round me as we watched the fat, barrel-like boat bob-glide into the turquoise-green harbour water. It was a tight squeeze through the narrow Ω gap of the harbour entrance, but it made it with an inch to spare and came to rest against the high-water walls. Its sails were faded red and its paintwork was bright like a circus caravan. It towed a much smaller boat behind, similarly decorated, riding high in the water because it was unladen.

In the stern of the fat boat the Collector sat on his blue canvas cushion with his hand on the tiller and he did not stand up until the prow of the boat had kissed hello to the harbour. Overhead the bunting fluttered in the breeze and the sunshine. Near the waiting bench the band played a medley of songs. It played some better than others.

Many people lined the harbour walls to look down on the Arrival of the fat boat and they applauded when the Collector finally rose to his feet. He swept off his hat with an extravagant bow to the assembled personages.

"My friends," he announced. "Once again I am touched by the warmth of your welcome."

And when he had replaced his hat he smiled, a big beaming smile, then made his way for'ard to ascend the rungs of the ladder and set foot on the quay.

IN THE SQUARE

In the Square he has erected a tent. The tent is square and the colour of cream. There are heavy brass eyelets with hairy ropes threaded through them. These ropes are tied off to anything which will accommodate them, which makes the tent a hazardous thing to navigate round, especially now it is dark.

Two flaps of canvas form the entrance of the tent and they do not quite meet in the centre. The tent is illuminated from within and the Collector's lamp casts silhouettes on the canvas so we can see the shapes of the Collector and anyone with him. Sometimes we can see the shapes of the things he is examining but sometimes they are too small or indistinct.

I am still with my father, standing in line outside the tent, waiting. I am not entirely sure why. Ahead of us in line there are Charlie and Francis and Livia Stevens and one or two others. Behind us there are more people, though some drift away or return with a thing they had forgotten. It is a long wait, but because I am with my father I do not mind. I had not expected it.

"Why are we here?" I ask my father.

"We're here because we don't belong there," he says simply. "Because we are unfinished. Except for you, Issy. You haven't started yet. Or maybe you have. I'm not sure. Sometimes it's confusing. That is the way of it."

"Started what?" I ask. "What is it I may or may not have started?"

"Ah," says my father, smiling as if he knows something. "Ask yourself the same question."

"I don't know the answer," I say after I have done that.

"Ask yourself later then," he says. "That often works."

In the distance I think I hear the sound of the gramophone playing. There are candles in jam jars around the edges of the square and the breeze makes them flicker in time with the waltzing tarantella from the gramophone. I look for Nancé but cannot see her.

IN THE TENT

We are inside the tent and the flaps fall closed behind us, though I do not remember passing through them.

Behind the collapsible table made of deal and baize the Collector beams at us. His be-ringed fingers lie still on the table before him. In the corner of the tent I see Patrice, sitting cross-legged with a book in front of him. He looks up but only for a moment, then returns to his reading.

At the Collector's table my father places a polished box of dark wood on the baize table top. He springs a catch and opens the lid.

"Ah," says the Collector when he sees the last metanism nested there with its polished carapace of copper and bronze and the single brass button, designed to be pressed.

"Father," I say.

He smiles at me, encouraging. "Do you see?"

I think I do see.

"It's a fine thing," says the Collector in his deep, theatrical voice. "A fine thing."

I think I see now and I reach out to close the box and take it from the table.

"Ah," the Collector says: a sigh of disappointment and resignation.

"I will go now," I tell my father, although I am sad to do so because it means leaving him again.

IN THE END

When I walk

                                               When I walked

out of the tent and into my room it will be

                       out of the tent and into my room it was

the morning and I will be

                                  the morning and I was

awake. It will be

                                          awake. It was

time to find Patrice.

DARK AND FAR

MONIA JA YKSI

A dozen years have passed. He is only known now by his title: *Hïr Aftstekt*.

The work has taken its toll. He has grown old, although in years he still would not be counted as such. In any mirror he sees the premature grey at his temples and in his beard. It is as if everything about him that was not the Count has fallen away to leave nothing but this brittle finger of ice and steel that is *Hïr Aftstekt*.

Periodically, measured by the moon and the tide, he is required to attend the Count, although his presence is merely symbolic. It is enough that he stands beside Him and can be seen by the crowd, tall and straight. In the shadows the tall dark men in hats are constantly present.

Beside Him, *Hïr Aftstekt* is impassive. This has always been his way. He has no facility for rhetoric, only numbers. This is his saving grace. When the address finally begins he calculates the meter of the speech.

"Ero on heikkoutta!

"Ero on virus, joka ei kuulu!

"Ero on ensimmäinen syöpäsolun!

"Stand up and be counted and I will tell you your number.

"Your number is En, for you are many and one.

"We are En-Mass!"

Hïr Aftstekt dissects each syllable and inflection and maps the pattern as a formula. The sum of it does not vary from the norm.

$$\infty/1 = \infty$$
$$\therefore \infty = en$$

As the En-Mass raise their fists in salute the torchlight glints from fifty thousand glass eyes – the eyes of the guess masks: flat and round.

They are worn now only as a symbol. The Errid has been banished by the Count, by the En-Mass.

AN UNDERSTANDING

Afterwards, as he left the platform down the turned concrete steps, the Architect stumbled, just for a moment, catching himself. The man in gabardine and silk waited below. He said nothing, although he had seen what had occurred. There was no need to speak. Over the many years they had developed an understanding, not dissimilar to the föhn wind.

"You should rest, *Hïr Aftstekt*," the man in gabardine and silk told him. "You are exhausted."

It was true that the Architect no longer found respite or relief in his sleep. Of late his dreams had been troublingly similar/vague. More often than not he woke thinking of cold, as if it was needed or necessary for something.

"Perhaps a break," the man in gabardine and silk continued, suggested. "Take some time away. Travel. Where would you like to go?"

The Architect considered this for some time. "I would like to cast for silverfish again," he said.

THREE

And so the Architect cast off the trappings of his office and travelled as anyone else would travel if they had a desire to reach the province of K_____. When he alighted from the train he alighted alone.

He took lodgings in a wooden house not far from the edge of town. He saw Bart as he walked there from the rail station but it had been so long since he had left that no-one recognised him. He did not jog their memories.

Once he had settled at the guest house he borrowed a fishing pole from the widow whose house it was and walked up to the hot pools to fish. Later, when he had grown stronger, he hiked up to the higher pools where the silverfish were bronze and the föhn wind was cool. Here, one day, he mounted a grassy outcrop and looked down at the plain to the east. On the open sweep of the grassland he saw the shapes of several sheds made small by the distance: a camp which he knew was not on any list.

In the evening he asked about the camp as he ate dinner at the guest house and the widow told him what she knew, which was not much.

Two days later the Architect left his lodgings early in the morning while the light was still grey. He had a rucksack on his back and carried a walking stick.

When he reached the high pools he paused to eat, then drank from his canteen and refilled it at the pool's edge, shooing away the bronze fish which were drawn to the movement. Afterwards he strode out down the slope towards the plain and at noon the ground beneath his boots had become flat.

Now he could not see the camp, for it was lost in the blur of the horizon, but he had a good fix on its direction and had calculated the number of steps he would make in order to reach it.

When he arrived it was late afternoon and there was some confusion until *Hïr Aftstekt* revealed his identity and asked to be given a tour of the camp.

In truth it was small – just two sheds and three huts – although the Supervisor kept it well organised and tidy. As he showed his visitor around he explained that the wire did not reach the camp (there had been a mistake in the plans when the camp was first constructed), but instead terminated two miles south. They had built a small shack there to protect the terminals.

The door of the last hut was painted yellow. Its occupants were at work in the sheds, save for one who sat quietly by a window.

When he saw the boy the Architect was still. The boy looked at him openly, calmly. He said nothing.

"Hello," said the Architect.

The boy said nothing.

"We think he's simple," the Supervisor said. "It's a shame. He's a good natured boy on the whole. Gets it from his mother is my guess. She was dandy."

The Architect looked at the boy and held up two fingers on his right hand. Then he closed the hand and held up one finger on his left hand.

The boy said and did nothing. After a moment the Architect lowered his left hand and smiled.

"Might I offer you tea?" the Supervisor asked.

"Of course," the Architect said. "Thank you."

But as they left the hut the Architect turned back for a last look at the boy and when he did so the boy held up a hand: three fingers.

PINCHBECK

When they returned to the city the Architect waited for the man in gabardine and silk to come to the apartment, but he did not.

After several days of waiting the Architect finally counted and knew that he would not see the man in gabardine again.

AN OPEN BOOK

"Patrice?"

The Architect stands over the boy who is reading by the firelight. The same book. It is a story about pirates and cargoes and jungle temples and gold. He is absorbed and does not look up.

"Patrice."

The Architect places a hand lightly on the book's open pages, breaking its spell on the boy so he does look up now.

"Two hundred and forty-two," the boy says calmly, looking into his father's face.

The Architect nods. "Go back to your book," he says softly.

N+1

Hïr Aftstekt gave out that his trip to the north had brought him a revelation. In his time there (he let them believe) he had seen the outline of a new design that was of such importance that it would provide the greatest step forward since Unification, since the En.

The Architect knew they would not question his assertion. How could they? The Leader was quite mad now, but the Count and the En were self-regulating and the tall dark men around the Leader knew this. They used it to their advantage. The Leader was maintained only as a puppet – an automaton, like Madam Scryer. He provided what was required for the small price of a token.

But all machines break in the end. *Hïr Aftstekt* knew this better than most. It would not be long.

So he did not try to be subtle or secret. Just the opposite. His activities (so he let them believe) were all driven by the New Work.

He consulted with physicists and philosophers when they could be found, for the truth was that few would own to such preoccupations any more. But when they were found he posed them all the same question and the answers he received varied as widely as random chance. Some would hold that yes, in the terms he laid out, such a thing *might* be possible; others would dismiss the notion – begging his pardon – as baseless and invalid: "Impossible, *Hïr*."

The only unequivocal answer he received was from a collector, whose activities were banned – strictly speaking – but who spoke loosely, such was his passion.

"I *know* such a thing is possible, *Hïr*," the man said. "For I have both seen it and felt it. Myself."

Whatever answers he received, *Hïr Aftstekt* sent his subjects away with tokens of appreciation, but without ever knowing whether they had satisfied him or not.

MADAM SCRYER

Now *Hïr Aftstekt* gave instructions. In the province of Sirte a factory complex was turned over to the production of thread so fine that it could not be seen, except in the light from a specially ground lens which itself took three months in the polishing. In four different towns he called upon printers – the last of the few – to set blocks of type which themselves were en-coded and meant nothing to those who impressed them on paper and sometimes on skins. And in the sugarbush plantations substantial rewards were offered to those who handed in the discarded carapaces of certain damselflies.

All this and more, and in his planning room the objects assembled and sat quiet in waiting. *Hïr Aftstekt* was like a man collecting for his death in the old way.

One day, on his way back to the apartment with a small wooden crate from a workshop in Qualm, *Hïr Aftstekt* noticed that his car had been driven into an area of the city which seemed vaguely familiar. He told the driver to stop for a moment so that he might cross the road to the fortune machine he saw on the corner.

It was many years since *Hïr Aftstekt* had visited this area of the city and many things had changed. One of the things which had not was Madam Scryer. Although the booth's paintwork was faded and chipped, inside the glass the mannequin was untouched by time.

The Architect took the third and last token from his pocket and thought of the man in gabardine and silk. He inserted the token.

When he gripped the handle the mannequin's movement began, and once the pantomime of writing was over a small card issued out of the machine. The card was light green and faded.

"*A pleasant memory of a happy incident in your life will be brought back to you by a meeting with an old friend in a few days' time...*"

Of course. The Architect remembered.

He placed the card in his pocket and returned to the car.

TAR

Hïr Aftstekt let it be known that he intended to inspect the sea defences. He set a date several weeks hence in order to show that there was no urgency to this, but that it was simply one duty amongst all the others, and so it was taken.

When the day came it was raining and the wipers moved jerkily across the windshield. Behind the partition *Hïr Aftstekt* held an open file on his lap but watched the passing view from the window and read only his thoughts.

On the beach road the convoy of cars came to a halt. It was still raining, though not hard, and the Architect waited for an assistant-guard to open the door and hold an umbrella as he stepped out.

He mounted the steps to the top of the concrete sea barrier and for a time he recorded measurements which he noted in a small book using a steel propelling pencil. The size and average shape of the shingle was determined. Samples were also taken, to return with them.

After an hour of this *Hïr Aftstekt* closed his pocketbook.

"I will walk for a while," he told the tall dark man who was closest to hand. "Before the return journey."

The tall dark man nodded.

Two hundred and three paces along the shoreline there was a rotting breakwater and in its lee sat an old man with his back to the planks. He was turning a small piece of flotsam in his fingers.

When the Architect stopped beside him the old man looked up without fear, which was a strange thing.

"I know you," he said.

The Architect studied the old man. Finally he said: "I know you too, Simian fisher. I thought you must be dead."

"Not yet, *Hïr*."

"And the others – the two who left with you? I forget their names."

"So do I," Simian fisher said. "They didn't make it."

For a moment the Architect considered the old man. "Perhaps I should buy you a drink."

The old man made a small bow of accession. "I wouldn't say no," he replied. "For old time's sake."

The Architect made a signal to his retinue, who always remained at the regulation distance, and started up the slope of the beach to the concrete wall. At the place where the shingle bank breeched the top he paused to let Simian fisher catch up and then they crossed the empty road to a bar and grill.

SALT

Inside they were alone. The tall dark men in hats had gone ahead and made sure of that.

The Architect chose a table by the window and did not speak until their drinks had been brought and the waitress had departed. They had a view of the damped seawall and the empty road and the bodyguards outside, as still as pins.

The Architect considered this view for a moment longer before turning to Simian fisher. There was an odour of damp salt and sand.

"What do you do here?" the Architect asked.

"As you saw, *Hïr*. I walk the beach behind the nets. I find things of interest and I leave them where I find them."

"What of the patrols?"

"They ignore me. They know I am harmless."

"They know nothing."

"Exactly."

"Ah," said the Architect, nodding.

Simian fisher drained his gin in a single swallow. When he replaced the glass on the table with a satisfied sound the Architect raised a hand and signalled to the waitress, then turned to consider the seawall while another drink was poured.

"Do you still think of it?" the Architect asked then.

Simian fisher chuckled.

"What is amusing?"

"That you and I are the same."

"Explain."

"We have made the same mistake."

"I doubt that," *Hïr Aftstekt* said.

The old man was still for a moment, then bowed his head in acknowledgment. "Yes, *Hïr*."

The Architect sipped his drink, though he barely allowed the liquid to wet his lips. He replaced his glass on the wooden table top and looked to the window. He was still as he contemplated the shore.

"I am an iron man, Simian: a grey man. The grey of polished steel and the sheen of oil. But when I think back to that place – to what it was like in the Far Lands – I see only colours."

"Yes, *Hïr*."

"Do any boats still leave?" the Architect asked.

Simian fisher shook his head. "There are many patrols, and the nets... I know about nets. They are tight. For a time I was employed in their repair. I was a skilled worker because I knew nets and most of them didn't. I taught them how to tie the knots so they would grow tighter with time. My knots are still out there." He gestured through the salt-grimed window to the invisible sea beyond the seawall. "I guess you could say they're my legacy, tied up with yours."

"So there are no boats," the Architect said.

"Who would risk it?" Simian fisher asked. "Who would believe anyway?"

"There must still be stories – fables; whispers; dreams."

"I couldn't say."

The Architect was silent then.

"What do you seek, *Hïr*?" the old man asked in the end.

The Architect said nothing.

"Will you tell me my numbers again? This time I would like to know."

"I doubt that," the Architect said. "Besides, don't you think there are enough numbers in the world without adding to them further?"

Simian fisher considered this for a while and concluded that it was true.

"So what do you seek, *Hïr*?" he repeated. "Really."

"You," said the Architect. "And a knowledge of nets and the tides."

"And a boat?"

"Could there be one?"

Simian fisher thought for some time. "Perhaps," he said in the end. – "If you wouldn't mind one that could use a lick of paint."

The Architect nodded. "Do you require anything?"

"Only gin and the shore," Simian said. "I have always maintained that gin is proof of the existence of God and the shore suits me fine."

"Very well," the Architect said and he rose from the table.

AS IT IS

In the counting sheds the tally sheets are collected, collated, calculated. Stubby white buttons on the Bakelite counting machines are depressed and small green circles from the green tally tickets cascade to the wooden floor. There is perfection in the bristles of the sweeping brush and the tin of the dustpan; in the smell of warm dust from the caged and studious lamps; in the hushed reverence and light perspiration of the enumerators; in the stub of yellow pencil.

In the dark waters of the docks, beside piers and amongst jetsam, their searchlights poke and probe. They sweep the oil-slicked water and illuminate the nets which now line every shore and every harbour to stop egress. There is perfection in the smell of tarred rope, drawn by the crank of a windlass; in the creak of a gunwale and the pitch darkness once the searchlight has passed; in the slop of water and the muttered oath of a deckhand.

AS IT SHOULD BE

In secret and in dark places he seeks the man and the woman. At first they are afraid and do not trust him. They fear that this is an elaborate trick – a means by which they will be led to betray themselves or others.

It is not until the Architect tells them why he wants this and shows them the boy through a part-open door that the man and the woman finally see that he has told them the truth.

"Will you do it?" he asks once the door has been closed quietly again.

The man and woman look at each other for a moment and then the man nods. "For the boy," the man says.

"That is all I ask."

"Will it— Will we be safe?" the woman asks. She puts a hand to the swell of her belly.

The Architect nods. "Everything will be as it should be," he tells her. "I am certain of that."

ASSEMBLY

Carefully the Architect assembles the components. Very carefully, with his long, dry fingers and a jeweller's loupe to his eye he works on the green baize of the table. At a certain stage in the construction he covers the partly completed object with a silk cloth while a servant brings in three buckets of ice, insulated with straw. The servant cannot help but cast an eye over the table.

"It is nothing," *Hïr Aftstekt* tells the man. But he knows that to the tall men in hats it will be nothing and something when they learn of this from the servant, as they surely will.

When the servant has left the room again the Architect uncovers the metanism and prepares it for the ice, which is something it requires for this stage if its construction to be complete. It requires cold.

TIN 6

"Patrice?"

The Architect stands over the boy, reading by the firelight. The same book. He is absorbed and does not look up. It is a story of clouds and high mountains and sacred objects, stolen.

"Patrice."

The Architect places a hand lightly on the book's open pages, breaking its spell on the boy so he does look up now.

"I must speak to you," The Architect tells him.

The boy continues to look, calmly. Then he says: "Nine... eight... seven. – Six."

"I know," says his father. "That is why you must listen. I must tell you a story."

BURLAP

The boy sleeps, but to be sure he will not wake he has been given a draught of green liquid disguised in his favourite drink, tasteless. Beside him his father glances at the sleeping face, illuminated only partly by the warm glow of the dashboard dials. The Architect wishes he could look for longer and perhaps perceive an answer which has eluded him. But he cannot risk taking his eyes from the road for more than a second or two. It is dark and there is a light rain. The blackout is tight.

When they arrive there is a moment of stillness once the car's engine has stopped. Then *Hïr Aftstekt* carries his son, cradled in his arms. Over the crushed shingle towards the cream of the slopping waves at the edge of the sea. Behind him he can hear the footsteps of Martin and Dot.

At the water's edge Simian fisher is waiting. He holds the knotted end of a rope which is fastened to a small boat with a furled sail and a pair of oars which move back and forth with the swell.

Without speaking The Architect wades into the water and carefully lowers the boy into the stern of the boat. He props the boy's head against the swollen cloth of a water sack, like a cushion. He adjusts the canvas bag around the boy's neck so that it sits flat against his chest. It contains the boy's book. It is a story of islands and shallow rivers and counting.

For a moment he looks at the sleeping boy and then the man and the woman are wading into the sea on the other side of the boat and the man is stowing their luggage: a seaman's kitbag and a small cardboard suitcase.

"Get in," Simian tells them in a low whisper. "Take the oars."

The man and woman do this. The man takes the oars and then Simian and *Hïr Aftstekt* push the boat off the shingle, propelling it seawards. No other words are spoken. They stand there without moving, watching as Martin pulls on the oars.

They stand there until they can no longer see the boat.

"How long will it take?" Simian fisher asks.

Hïr Aftstekt shakes his head. "I cannot count."

(N)ONE

When they came for him later, as he had known they would, they saw that *Hïr Aftstekt*'s shoes were wet, as if he had been standing in a river, or in the sea.

"I would very much like to retire to the camp," *Hïr Aftstekt* told them.

The tall dark man in a hat nodded. "That can be arranged, but I very much doubt you will get there."

The Architect acknowledged that with a nod and a sigh. "May I? A last look...?"

His gesture was to the long, green baize table, still laid out with the collected objects. In the straw-insulated buckets the ice had finally melted.

The tall dark man nodded curtly and the Architect moved to stand beside the table. His long, dry fingers caressed the baize and oak like glass for a moment, then the Architect drew aside the black silk cloth which covered the metanism. There was no showmanship in this action for the Architect was no conjurer, but nor did he hesitate in what he must do.

With a delicate finger the Architect pressed a small, polished brass button in the centre of the metanism's back. Immediately it commenced to make a small ticking sound. This drew the attention of the tall dark man.

"What have you done?"

The Architect said nothing. He took a step back.

Two wings sprang from the carapace of the metanism, their surfaces interlaced with a thread so fine it could not be seen without a specially ground lens. The wings beat and the metanism rose up, chattering and whirring softly.

The tall dark man snatched off his hat and swatted at the metanism, trying to catch it, but failing.

"What have you *done*?" he cried.

More tall dark men entered quickly when they heard the first man's alarm. They also set to, swatting and trying to catch the metanism in their hats. The Architect smiled at this sight. As the metanism whirled out into the night through the open window the Architect bit down on the capsule he had placed between his teeth. In the metanism's departing breeze he already felt the sensation it bore. It was............ *Release*.

As he tasted the bitterness on his tongue the Architect stopped counting. It was............ *Dandy*

PATRICE

IN THE END (REPRISE)

When I walked out of the tent and into my room it was the morning and I was awake. It was time to find Patrice.

THE BIRDS ARE FLOWN

A skein of black crows flew west across the blue and cloud sky as I walked to ap-Huish. I knew that was where I would probably find Patrice, still and again. In a field I saw a magpie hop down from the back of a sheep to retrieve something from the earth, then return to its perch. The magpie turned a marble eye towards me as I passed and I said, as is the custom, "*Hej-hej, Herra Fyrsta Fuglur.*"

The magpie dipped his head. Very well.

When I reached ap-Huish beach I made for the rusted ring in the rock and looked to see if there was a water clock and a piece of string there. There was not. I looked out across the water to Huish and cupped my hands to my mouth and called Patrice's name in two elongated syllables: "Paaat-reeece!"

I waited and there was no response. I saw no movement of a human kind. The sea breeze was a constant thing, bending the grass of the dunes east to west. It had ripped Patrice's name to shreds as soon as it left my cupped hands.

I sat down on the sand and thought hard about what I should do.

FLUX

I knew it was for me to do now, and no one else. I could feel it like the ache of a missing toe, and like the weight of a sack on my back. *It has come to this*, I thought to myself. *It has come to me, now that the Flying Horse Tea Room is closed and people have built a raft and left a gramophone sitting on the cobbles.*

I knew things were not as they should be. There was no doubt about that. I was impatient for this state of affairs to be resolved. I had started to dislike the fact that things were not as they were. I wanted things to be the same as they had been; or if not, then to know what they would become. Quickly. I did not like the feeling that everything was betwixt and between one state of affairs and another.

When I was a smaller girl my father taught me how to solder two pieces of metal together by melting a third to bridge the gap between them. It is a very satisfying thing to do, the combination of heat and flux and melting silver metal followed by the hiss of quenching. The run of the solder and the hiss of the quench were the parts I liked best.

I felt I should do something like that now, but I wasn't sure how.

I wished that I could talk to Sam Hall because he would be slow to think about it and consider it in full. I wished I had brought some of the left-over cake from the Tea Dance instead of feeding it all to the chickens.

In the end none of these wishes could come true. It was too late for that. I decided that whatever I did now would have to be made into the correct thing to do because there was no other choice.

I unfastened the buckles on my shoes and took off my shoes. Then I stood up from the sand and lifted my skirt and waded out into the water towards Huish.

ON HUISH AGAIN

It felt strange to be on Huish again without the pull of the string tied to my finger and without the collecting tin for the coast sloes. As I passed I saw that the sloes were not as salty as before. I had already picked all the best ones. I didn't know if this meant anything.

Through the dune grass tickling at my ankles I went to the place where I had seen the nearly boat. It wasn't there.

What was there was a shallow groove in the sand which I took to be the mark of the nearly boat's keel as it had moved or been moved through the dunes. The breeze was still strong enough to tear up any words so I didn't call any. I followed the nearly boat's track in the sand instead, seeing that in places the dunes were already shifting to cover it up.

I followed the track around and up and over the dunes, past a place where a low square wall of bricks was filled with egg-sized pebbles and surrounded by sand. From there I could see out across the whole wide expanse of the ocean. I shaded my eyes with my hand. The ocean went on for ever. It was very bright.

I lowered my hand and my gaze. On the beach in front of the ocean I saw the nearly boat half in and half out of the water, as if it was deciding. Sitting on the plank across the centre of the boat I saw Patrice staring out to sea as if he was considering.

"HELLO, PATRICE,"

I said.

He jumped when I said it. He turned around quickly and stood up awkwardly. The nearly boat rocked. I saw that the knot holes in her sides had all been filled with pegs carved from sweet amelia, no doubt to make her seaworthy again. She was a boat once again.

I saw a look of relief on Patrice's face. I could tell he was very glad to see me and I was glad about that because it is always pleasant to be welcome.

"Issy," he said. "I'm very glad to see you."

"I'm pleased to find you, too," I told him, which was true. I was pleased that I had found him so expeditiously, rather than having to spend who-knew-how-long searching. If he hadn't been here I wasn't sure where else I would have gone to look.

"I see you've repaired the nearly boat," I told him. The boat's hull was like one of Nancé's pin cushions, bristling with the pegs.

NO CHOICE AT ALL

"I don't know where I should go," Patrice told me then.

I could see it was a terrible thing for him, his not knowing. I could see that it was like the ache of a missing toe, or like the weight of a sack on his back.

He stepped out of the boat and came to sit beside me on the dry sand while I thought.

"I think we have three choices," I told him. "First choice: we can go back to the is-Lands, but I have just come from there and I do not think it will help."

Patrice shook his head at that notion. He seemed very set against that choice even though he didn't say anything, but waited to hear the other options.

"Second choice: we can stay here, although I do not think that's a very practical idea, unless we eat nothing but coast sloes."

Again Patrice shook his head, although with slightly less vehemence, I noted.

"In that case there is only one choice, which makes it no choice at all," I told him. "We must set sail in the repaired boat."

When I said this Patrice pointed out that we could not set sail because there was no sail – not even a mast – on the repaired boat. I told him rather exasperatedly that I had been speaking metaphorically and that we would have to row instead (there *were* oars). I wanted to concentrate on the idea rather than being side-tracked by the presence or lack of a sail.

Patrice didn't not look very sure of the idea. "Is there no other way?" he asked.

I told him that I couldn't think of one. I thought we had no choice.

"Where do you think it will get us?"

"Wherever it is, it's not back and also not here," I said with a shrug. "That is the only place we *can* get to. It's as simple as that."

Patrice still did not seem convinced and I seem to remember there was a

SHORT INTERLUDE

which may have been brief, but also long enough to encompass me walking a little way along the beach and paddling in the water. I seem to remember that I picked up a shell. I seem to think that I felt warm in the sunlight and as if I had eaten an egg sandwich, although I have no idea where such a sandwich might have come from. Perhaps there was a hamper in the dunes beside a tartan rug with a tasselled fringe, set out for a picnic. The breeze would have blown sand grains across the rug.

There may, too, have been a lying on my back with my eyes closed and feeling sleepy in the sunlight before returning to the repaired boat. All these things, it seemed were

RUNNINGTOGETHER

in an. Odd way. I*was*onHuishafter-all.

SHOWN

Whatever had or not happened in the interlude, Patrice still did not seem able to cut his knot to the here. I took the polished cube of a box from my pocket – which I had only recently remembered, but not how it was there – and held it out flat on the palm of my hand.

When I opened the box Patrice gazed at the metanism inside it. Then he squinted. Then he frowned. I said nothing. Neither did he. I waited and as I knew that he would, Patrice extended a finger to the small pressable button in the centre of the metanism's back.

There was a small ticking sound, which made Patrice snatch his hand back. But he did not take his eyes off the metanism as its wings sprang into place and whirred and beat upwards, spiralling round.

The sunlight burnished the brass and the copper as the metanism described circles over our heads. Then it hovered there.

I saw the feeling of release come over Patrice

"Hold out your hand," I told him, and he did.

The metanism came down. It alighted on the pads of his fingers. It folded its wings. It was still. After a moment I lifted it gently back into its box.

"Shall we go now?" I asked.

Patrice nodded. There was release.

FINE FOR A WHILE

Now we were ready to go Patrice moved to the bow of the repaired boat, which in my head I had named *Sweet Amelia* on account of her repairs. I knew that once she was fully in the water the pegs in her holes would swell and fit even more snugly.

I pushed *Sweet Amelia* off from the sand and when she was fully floating she seemed at once to have an enthusiasm and zest for the journey, like a dog (I imagine) which has been kept inside for a long time. It doesn't mind where it is taken, it is just glad to know it will be able to run.

I climbed in over *Sweet Amelia*'s stern and felt her quiver. We were already moving away from the beach, despite there being no sail and no mast. The wind was behind us and I had to move briskly to secure the oars in their locks and take up position to row. Patrice asked if he should move to the stern now, but I told him he was fine where he was for a while. I was quite relieved that things seemed to have stopped running together as soon as we left the beach.

AT SEA

As I rowed my confidence in *Sweet Amelia* grew. I felt that she knew where she was going and that she was confident we would want to go there, too. I believed she was eager to please and to demonstrate that – despite all her repairs and the sad state of her paintwork – she was, even yet, a vessel to be reckoned with.

So I didn't row hard or concern myself overly much with our direction. Despite all that had happened during and then after the Tea Dance I felt soothed by the zesty enthusiasm of *Sweet Amelia*, and by the rhythm of the rowing through the smoothly undulating green of the sea as it slipped past the sides of our boat. I could imagine the clear little bow-wave riding up against the stem post, although – of course – I couldn't see that.

Every now and then I turned to look at Patrice who was watching ahead of us, so all I could see was the back of his head. But I thought that he, too, seemed to be feeling something different. I wondered if I should ask him about the noose I had seen hanging from the tree at the north corner of the Square. It seemed clear that he knew something about it, but although I was curious about his escape, I felt it wouldn't be right to ask him directly. I didn't want to disturb him with painful memories of torches in the darkness and hands and ropes and the crowd clawing at him. Who knew who they were? They were one and all and that was enough.

Our little wake giggled and gurgled behind us and the oar blades made small white vortices in the clear water.

ON WHELME

We were progressing around the shore of Whelme is-Land as the sun came on to evening. Patrice had taken a turn at the oars. Although he wasn't a very skilled oarsman I knew it was important that he should feel himself a part of this enterprise, so I didn't offer advice except occasionally.

As it came on to evening I told Patrice that I thought we should stop for the night. I pointed to a place where *Sweet Amelia* might nuzzle up to the sand, rather than rocks, and when we were ashore there I tied her painter securely to the bough of an overhanging tree.

The grass there on Whelme was lush and dark and dewed. Bluebells edged out of shaded hedges. Wrens trilled. It was the end of the kind of Spring day which has taken you by surprise with the warmth of it and made you take off your cardigan or sweater which hadn't been as necessary as you thought it would be some hours before.

We were hungry and thirsty by then, so I sought out the path to Joby Carter's caravan. When we found it it led us past the wood of silver birch trees, tall and spindly in their birch way. When we reached the red fingerpost I stopped and said: "Let's take a diversion. There is something I think you should see."

LAST WORDS

The sandy path led shortly to a grove in the birches. Here, between the trunks of the trees, there were ropes and string and twine and thread from which hung barrels and buckets and tin cans and thimbles. There was a sigh in the air between the branches and leaves, although the air was very still.

All the varied receptacles hung with their open mouths downward, as if trapping air under water. This was something similar to what they did do, although they did not trap air and it was not under water. They trapped words and it was under the air.

Patrice looked curiously at these varied receptacles. He did not know, so I explained.

"It is a part of Library," I told him. "An annexe. This is the Catalogue of Last Words. Here, let me show you."

I moved to a galvanised pail which was conveniently close to the path through the bluebells. It hung from a stout, hairy string. I used both hands to hold it steady and pressed my ear against its cool metal side.

"...It wasn't so bad. It wasn't so good either, truth be told, but hell, at least it was something. *Can't say more than that. Wish I could."*

"You try it," I told Patrice.

Somewhat cautiously he moved to an oil drum and did as I had done, pressing his ear against it. After a second he recoiled back in surprise.

"What did you hear?"

"I don't think I can say. It was an expletive."

"Ah," I said. "Sometimes it is."

Patrice thought about that for a moment. "How do you *know* all these things?" he asked then.

"I was born here," I told him. "And my father always encouraged me to have the Pleasure Of Finding Things Out."

JOBY CARTER

We listened to more last words, but we were still hungry and thirsty so after a short time we went back to the main path and followed it some more until we came to Joby Carter's caravan which sat in a clearing surrounded by found bottles and pails and anything which had the capacity for last words.

Joby Carter sat on the step of his caravan, patching a bucket which he held between his knees.

Joby Carter was an exceptionally ugly man, but it was the kind of ugliness which is fascinating to observe. He reminded me a little of Sam Hall, although Joby was unpleasantly fat and not stick-thin like Sam. Perhaps he only reminded me of Sam because they both lived away from others and may not really have wished to do so.

Although Joby was ugly, the longer you observed him, the stranger was the result. Because after a while you began to see that Joby was not ugly at all. True, he was still no oil painting, but his ugly features began to take on a much more familiar and appealing form, so that in the end you did not think he was ugly; he was just Joby and you could get on with the business of being with him.

SUPPER

Joby put his bucket aside and made supper when I told him we were hungry and thirsty. We all ate from birch bowls with birch spoons.

As we ate I explained to Joby that Patrice and I were on a journey by boat and what had occasioned it. He expressed a polite interest when I told him about the Tea Dance and Afterwards, but I could tell that it was only out of politeness and not really enthralment, so I cut the long story short. Very short.

"Things aren't right," I told him.

He shrugged. "All's right here," he said, losing interest in that.

I knew from past experience that Joby would be more interested in doing the rubbing of the bodies thing with me, but I hadn't decided if I wanted to get on to *that* at this moment – or at a later one. Perhaps I needed to observe him for a little while longer, so he became more familiar. He and Sam Hall were at opposite ends of the spectrum to be sure.

I could see that Patrice had been observing Joby for a long time now, and that he was starting to see that Joby was not as ugly as he had first appeared.

By the time we had eaten supper it was dark and Joby showed Patrice to a hammock, slung between birch trees, where he could sleep at the edge of the clearing.

Joby and I sat for a little while longer, outside the caravan on the ground.

"You and him," he said gesturing at Patrice. "You got something going there?"

I told him that we had some*where* to be going, if that's what he meant.

He nodded. "How about that Sam Hall, then?" he asked. "What's going there?"

Once a once a time Joby and Sam had been friends, but Joby liked to argue and Sam did not, so they parted.

I told Joby that I liked visiting Sam Hall on Hallows is-Land and that I had promised to go there again soon.

Joby sighed.

His belly was a large rounded hill, at rest in the landscape under the moon, with a moonpool belly button at its summit. I smoothed my hand down it's fine roundness and remembered laying myself over it, as if laying myself over the land, accepting its contours.

I knew it was what Joby wanted again, and in some ways I knew I would enjoy the feeling of laying myself over the world-hill of his belly. But I did not.

"If it's any consolation, I think your belly is as round as Colmer's Hill," I told him.

He sighed again then.

"Is that any consolation?" I asked and after a while he said that it was.

"A good night to you, Joby," I said.

"Thank you, Issy," he said.

In the morning, after breakfast, Patrice and I returned to *Sweet Amelia*, who had waited patiently by the shore, and we set off again.

THE MIST

When the mist came it settled over our *Sweet Amelia* like a rain cloud without rain and there was no way to tell whether we sat in the middle of a small cloud which moved with us for company, or whether we moved through a large cloud which did not move at all. At different times I believed each possibility with equal conviction.

Patrice did not like the mist, I could tell, but he did not say so. He did not say very much. When we did speak in the mist our voices seemed to lack velocity and the words seemed to fall on to the damp planks of *Sweet Amelia*'s hull and wriggle there like small fish, surprised and confused at finding themselves in the wrong element.

After a day of the mist I was no longer sure whether we were travelling inwards or outwards or neither. I no longer felt the pull of the is-Lands – or rather, I felt that I no longer felt something which I had always felt in the past but had been so accustomed to feeling that it was only now, when I didn't feel it, that I knew it *had* been there and now wasn't.

Patrice no longer wanted to row. He feared rocks in the mist. He spent long times staring out over the bow. I knew that his brow would be creased with looking.

When night came I dreamed of a Departure. As far as I knew, no one had ever dreamed of a Departure before, but I dreamed it in the same way the Siisters dreamed of an Arrival, but exactly the reverse. Which could only mean that it *was* a dream of Departure, even though no one I knew had ever dreamed such a thing before.

When I woke up from the dream I saw that the mist had lifted and there was clear sky and stars above us and *Sweet Amelia* was perfectly still. Because I hadn't seen the mist leave there remained no way to know whether it had been a small cloud (moving), or a very large one (still). One or other of us had drifted away.

A HOLE IN THE OCEAN

We had been one day and one night at sea now and in the morning I rowed again. As I rowed I could feel that *Sweet Amelia* was moving more easily than she had through the mist. I could feel that there was a current drawing her along, as well as the bite of the oars in the water.

"What is that?" Patrice said.

I turned on the seat to look where Patrice was pointing. There was a hole in the ocean.

The hole was like a well: perfectly round. Above it there was a cloud of mist from the waters as they tumbled over and into the well wall. In one or two places I could see flotsam and jetsam stuck against the sunken top of the wall. I guessed that the depth of the water flowing over the top of the wall might not be very great; perhaps only a matter of inches.

Beside the hole there was a rusted steel structure like a stove pipe poking out of the swell.

As we drew closer I could see that it wasn't really a stove pipe at all. It was much more like a tower rising out of the sea. It was large enough to accommodate five or six people if they all stood with their backs to each other, as if they'd had a disagreement. If five or six people stood like that, each one would have had a porthole to look out of. The portholes were arranged neatly in the lovely rusted sides of the tower, very high up. There was also a hatch from which a ladder came down many feet to a steel landing place.

As we drew closer to the tower I didn't need to row. *Sweet Amelia* was tugged along by the current of water being drawn over the edge of the well. She seemed keen to explore the waterfall place, but I was concerned that we might get in deeper than she imagined, so I dug deep with the oars and directed *Sweet Amelia* towards the landing stage beside the tower, although she was reluctant to go.

All around the tower there were barnacles and marks from the tides. All was rust and it was lovely.

A TOWER IN THE SEA

"What should we do now?" Patrice asked.

Ever since we had left Whelme I had noticed that he only asked questions. He was relying on me more and more to tell him what he should do.

"We should tie up here," I told him. "Can you tie up the rope?"

He tied the painter line to a slender pole rising vertically from the corner of the landing platform.

"Is that good enough?" he asked. I said that it was.

"We should climb up," I told Patrice before he could ask what we should do next. "I will go first; you follow me."

As I climbed the ladder I counted the rungs: 33.

At the top of the ladder I held on to the last rung with one hand and reached to the handle of the hatch with the other. Once the hatch was unlatched I had to descend three rungs so it could swing open over my head. It was an awkward arrangement for coming and going, I thought.

A ROOM IN THE TOWER

When we climbed inside we found a room in the tower, with a steel plate floor and polished wood benches lining the curved walls. It smelled of tobacco and leather and salt.

Inside we also found aüggie, although he looked different. He had not a tooth in his head and his yellow hair hung like thatch to his eyebrows as if it was straw. I would not have been surprised to see a swallow fly out from beneath it. This made me think that he was not aüggie, but I wasn't sure.

"You just arrived?" notaüggie asked. He was involved in something with his hands and a long strip of leather and knots.

I told him we had and made introductions and told how we had come here after a day in the mist, and now we weren't sure of our bearings or how far from the is-Lands we might be.

Notaüggie listened to this and didn't look entirely happy that we were there. He had the impatient look of a man who is bothered by strangers who turn up announced and distract him from what he is doing. He told us his name was Aüggie and reacted quite sharply I thought when I asked if he had a brother perhaps. He said no.

RAIN AND CRANKS

It started to rain as we were talking this way. We heard it as a soft, random plinking on the steel roof. At first no one noticed because the sound was so soft, but when Aüggie noticed the sound it immediately sent him into a flurrious frenzy of activity.

He pushed past us – the space was rather cramped – and moved to the polished handle of a crank and began to turn it vigorously. Overhead I heard the shifting of plates although I couldn't see what it was that was shifting. After he had cranked the crank Aüggie then moved quickly round the room, opening little brass taps connected to thin copper tubes which rose to the ceiling. Suspended in a cradle under each tap was a glass bottle, though they didn't all match.

Soon rainwater began to flow from the taps and drip into the bottles suspended below. There were twelve bottles and each one began to fill.

"Can't waste it," Aüggie said catching his breath after his exertions. "Can't waste a drop."

He reminded me of someone, but I couldn't say who.

Once he was satisfied that all the bottles were filling up, Aüggie relaxed a little. All we could do now was wait for the rain to cease. As I watched the level of the water slowly rise in each bottle I wondered what would happen if they became full to over-flowing and I asked that question.

"Never happens," Aüggie said, so I watched the bottles carefully as each one was filled.

In a while the rain stopped. The cloud was discharged. Each bottle was now full to within a thumb's width of the top but none had overflowed, just as Aüggie had predicted.

Now he went around the room with methodical movements. He corked each bottle in turn and removed it to a crate stuffed with straw, taking out a new, empty bottle to make space. He placed the new, empty bottle in the vacant cradle beneath the tap. He did this twelve times.

"So," Aüggie said when he had finished. "Tell me the story."

I thought it was better perhaps if I waited until Patrice was asleep. He was yawning and tired and when I commented on that he asked if he should go to sleep. I told him I thought he should, which he did. He stretching out on the steel floor of the round room on cushions from a few of the side benches. Aüggie said he might use them.

When I was sure Patrice was asleep I began to tell Aüggie the/this story.

THE STORY/AFTERWARDS

At an intermission in the story Aüggie offered to make cordial and I accepted gratefully because my throat had become dry from telling. Aüggie made the cordial with precision and smacked his lips over his toothless gums when he had sipped it all down.

"Go on now," he said.

After the intermission I continued the/this story. When I reached the end/now I stopped.

Aüggie blinked at me.

"It isn't finished," he complained, a little too quickly I thought. I was a little annoyed that he didn't seem to appreciate that I had put in the details and talked myself dry (twice now) for his benefit. I decided to keep quiet for a while so that he would have time to reconsider.

"Well," he said in the end. "There are things to be attended to. The amount of work I got these days, if I took time out for unfinished story listening all the time I'd never keep on schedule. You people don't realise. Place won't run itself, I'm not there."

He stood up.

"Which people?" I asked.

"Tall men in dark hats for a start," he told me. "Personally I don't have much time for them but it's gotta be done."

He was already opening the trap door in the floor as he said this. As it opened I smelled the faint odour of oil and steam and cracked ozone.

"What should I do?" I asked. I got to my feet because I was a little afraid that this was and wasn't the end of the story at the same time. It also occurred to me that now I was also asking everything as a question, just like Patrice. There seemed no way around it, even though I had little faith in Aüggie as someone with answers.

"Finishing that story of yours would be a start," he said. "Some kinda resolution would be good."

"But—?" I said.

But there was no but because he had gone through the trap door and it had closed behind/over him.

NIGHT & SOUNDS

I was at a loss what to do. My mind was full of questions but I couldn't think of any answers. I wondered if we should leave? I wondered if there was anything to eat? I wondered how long Aüggie would be away and if he would come back?

I went to one of the portholes nearest to the hatch and unscrewed it so I could look out and down. When I looked down the length of the ladder outside I saw that the landing platform was submerged now because the tide had risen. There were four feet of clear, swollen water above the landing stage. There was no sign of *Sweet Amelia*. She must have slipped her painter. Had she abandoned us now?

It was getting dark now and there was little else I could do. I took some more cushions from the seats and put them on the floor beside Patrice, then I lay down beside him. He was asleep still and soon I was too?

?

"Oh, all right then," Aüggie said as if we had been conversing for some time before this point and somehow I had succeeded in convincing him – against his better judgement, it had better be said – that something I had proposed was the best thing to do.

"All right then what?" I asked. I had only just been woken by Aüggie's return to the room in the tower. It was morning.

"I'll take him."

"You will?"

"That's what I said and I'm a man of my word."

He sounded tetchy and although I didn't know to what he was referring I was afraid that if I asked another question (and it seemed that there would be no alternative) he would take it entirely the wrong way. Then I was afraid he would change his mind about whatever thing he had agreed to do.

I had a hard time waking Patrice. When he did wake he continued to have the look of someone who has not entirely stepped out of the sleep they were having.

"Are we leaving?" he asked.

"Would you like to?" I asked.

"Where are we going?" he asked.

"Does it matter?" I asked.

"All of us?" He looked at Aüggie as he asked that.

"Would you like us all to go?"

Patrice looked dazed. I could see him struggle to find a response.

He said: "Have you ever had the feeling you would like to make a statement, but that something has got hold of that part of your tongue and makes everything a question instead?"

I knew I couldn't give him an answer but I did have that feeling.

"Well come on then," Aüggie said, raising the trap door. "Let's get it done, shall we?"

"Oh, don't *you* start," I told him. That felt better.

DOWN

We went down, inside the tower in the sea. The air there was cold and the sound of our feet on the iron-winding steps echoed off the rust-red steel walls. There was light from a lamp on a chain in the centre of the tower which Aüggie pulled down as we went, using a stick which seemed to have been made for this purpose. We went down in a bubble of light.

No one spoke. It was impossible to know how far we had come or how far to go unless you counted the steps, which I tried, but after three I always lost count. I wondered if this was the same for Patrice. He had not mentioned any numbers since we had set out on this journey. In fact, now that I thought about it because there was nothing else to think about, I didn't think I could remember him saying any number since we'd met in the library beside his map of the is-Lands when I hadn't liked him very much. If at all.

We went down, round and round. Aüggie went first, then Patrice. I was the last. I kept my hand on the rough rope hung round the wall of the tower. Every three and three and three steps there was a knot in the rope which made my hand bump.

AT THE BOTTOM

At the bottom, when I stepped off the last step, I found it hard to walk in a straight line for several moments because we had been going round and round for so long.

IN THE WELL OF THE SEA

We were in a corridor now. Aüggie unhooked his stick from the lamp on the chain and re-hooked the stick to a lamp near the roof which was mounted on a small metal track. When Aüggie moved forward he dragged the light with him and we went forward in a bubble of light.

I would have said something now because I felt that I could say it without it being a question (although it would have been a question because that was what I wanted to say). But I didn't say anything for two reasons. One was that Aüggie had not paused when he dismounted the steps, the other was that anything I had said would not have been heard.

A huge tremblingrumbling sound filled the air and I knew we must be close to the hole in the ocean and that the sound must be caused by the falling of water inside it.

This was proved true a little time later when Aüggie led us past an opening in the rock wall, beyond which was a curtain of white and blue water. Odd droplets of water splashed back at us and there was a puddle on the rock floor. We had to paddle through it to continue our journey.

THE TURBINE HALL

We went as far as was necessary for the sound of the falling water to decrease enough to speak (though no one did) and then we entered a room.

It was a large room and very well lit. It was so bright that there were no shadows anywhere. The floor was as smooth as glass and of a light green colour. It matched the enamelled metal of the large, circular boxes – four of them – which were equally spaced out down the length of the room. These boxes all emitted a light hum of slightly different pitches and warm air flowed gently from vents in their sides.

"Them's the turbines," Aüggie said with evident satisfaction, as if he knew he had guessed my question.

I pretended I knew what he meant. Then wished I hadn't. There was a lot I didn't understand about this place. Almost everything, in fact. But Aüggie acted as if we had come here knowing what we would find and so he didn't seem to feel the need to explain or offer a commentary. I wished Patrice would ask a question, but he hadn't spoken since we left the top of the tower in the sea. In fact, neither had I.

I cleared my throat, by way of an experiment. I said: "Where do we go now?"

It sounded the same as I had hoped that it would.

"You?" Aüggie said. "You don't go nowhere. Not you. Not now. Only the boy. That's what was agreed."

"Agreed?"

"One ticket, that's all."

He rummaged in a pocket and pulled out a faded green card, holding it out.

I read: *A pleasant memory of a happy incident in your life—*

I couldn't read any more before Aüggie put it away.

"You got a ticket you haven't told me about?" he asked. He sounded suspicious.

I confessed I had not.

"That's it, then," Aüggie said. It was decided. "That far. No farther."

He gestured to the end of the room where there was a doorway of sorts, and what looked like more steps.

Did he mean no farther or no father? I looked at Patrice to see if he understood any of this better than me. It didn't seem that he did.

"Patrice?" I asked.

He shook his head.

LIKE FATHER, LIKE FAR

At the end of the turbine hall I could go that far and no farther. There was a doorway, an arch, cut in the rock with steps going down to another, long room.

Aüggie did not pause at the top of the steps but continued on down as if he had a schedule to keep and we had delayed him already. On the floor, I saw then, was a yellow line.

I wanted to step over this line and carry on (although I had no ticket) but then Patrice touched my arm.

"Thank you for coming this far," he told me.

"I could come farther," I said.

I was curious to see more and I hadn't quite liked the way Aüggie had told me I needed a ticket, which I was quite sure I did not.

Patrice shook his head. "I think you should stay in the Far Lands," he said. "You were born here."

The toe of his shoe scuffed the paint of the line on the floor.

What could I do? I wasn't at all sure that I should let Patrice go on alone, but he seemed certain that it was for the best.

"Goodbye, Issy," he said, stepping over the line. He went down the steps quickly, as if to make up for the delay.

"Goodbye, Patrice," I told him, but by then he wasn't there, and neither was Aüggie. I thought I heard a steel door close in the distance, but it was too late to tell. And so that was that.

THE WEIGHT

It was hard to tell what I should do now. There was no one to ask. I couldn't go farther, that was for sure, which meant I could only stay or not stay. It wasn't much of a choice. I would have liked something more. I was under the ocean and I felt that the weight of water above me was pressing down on my ribs, like lying down on a bed with a cat purring on your chest in the sunlight. I had to remind myself to breathe in.

ON THE EBB TIDE

When I left the turbine room it wasn't the same as the way we had come. For some reason.

I turned left and then right. Which was not right, even though I had left.

After not very long in a low corridor I came to a small doorway which I went through and emerged on a ledge with a rusted steel railing. It was a tunnel: very high. Very. I could not see the roof. Below there was a canal of cloudy water, like turquoise milk where lights like fallen leaves on Hallows drifted in a slow silent procession. The lights moved very slowly. Very. They flowed like the last of an ebb tide which never turns.

After I had watched the lights floating past slowly for as long as I could I saw that there was a bridge further up stream. So I walked along the ledge with my hand on the rail until I came to the bridge where the ledge stopped.

There was a yellow line on the ledge at the start of the bridge but it was very scuffed and hard to see. Very. It was so hard to see that you might not have seen it was there at all, so I felt I could safely go on.

JUST PASSING THROUGH

I was surprised, but not very, to see – when I stepped on to the bridge – that there was someone quite near the centre.

He was a tall man – quite thin – who looked as if he would be comfortable with numbers and a pencil in his long fingers. He was looking down at the canal below as if counting the lights, but perhaps he wasn't – counting that is – because he did not look as if he had lost count when he looked up and saw me.

"Hello. Who are you?" I said, because I wanted to be polite.

He gave that some thought.

"At the moment I am not quite certain," he replied. I saw that he used his hands as much as his voice to communicate. There was a strange absence of sound in some of the things he said.

"I'm Issy, which is short for Isadora," I said. "Do you live here?"

He paused to give that some thought, too, then his hands fluttered again and said: "I think I am just passing through."

"That makes two of us, then," I told him.

HOW TO COUNT

We stood for several moments after I'd said this, as if he was trying to remember if I had said it aloud.

"I have been" *indirectly responsible* "for many" *bad* "things," he half said with his voice and half with his hands.

He paused to look at the slow water below before resuming again.

"As I say, I have been a facilitator of things which should not have happened. I do not know – individually – what they may have been. I only know that they must have occurred. It is an easy enough calculation to make. In my defence I can say only that in some small ways I have, I think, done some good, also." *At least, I have tried.*

I nodded because I understood this. "It's the thought that counts," I told him.

He shook his head gravely. "No. My thought *was* the Count, but the end result was the En-Mass." *It is painful to me.*

I waited for him to say more because he seemed rueful. He looked at me curiously then, as if realising I was there. "You don't know of these things?"

"I know *how* to count," I told him.

"Where are you from?"

"I'm from the is-Lands," I told him. "I was born on Whelme and then lived on Fryst with my father because he needed the cold for the things he was making. Lately I was on Faer is-Land, to live with the Siisters, but now that they're disappointed I'm not sure where I will go. Yet."

"The islands?" he said, as if he had stopped listening forty-eight words ago.

"Yes, the is-Lands," I said.

"Please, tell me about them," he said.

So I did.

As I told him about the is-Lands I saw that he was remembering or perhaps daydreaming of such a place. I'm not sure he knew which.

In the end he said simply, "So, it wasn't for nothing."

Then his hands moved, which meant *I am happily relieved.*

There was such a release in his face that I thought – for a moment – that the metanism might have flown free of its box in my pocket, but when I felt for the box it was still there and still closed.

THE SENSE OF AN ENDING

In the water below us luminous fish trailed lazy fins in the slow current, unless startled by some imaginary disturbance. Then they darted all of a sudden before calming again.

I knew that an ending was very close. I could sense it. I didn't know how long it would take to arrive. I didn't know whether it was close because I had moved towards it, or whether it was moving toward me. I didn't know if it was *my* ending or whether it belonged to someone else and I had just happened across it, as you can happen upon a sheep on Jawbones Hill during a walk. You meet the sheep but it pays you no attention because it isn't your sheep and it has other plans in mind.

Perhaps the ending I sensed had other plans in mind, also.

TIME TO GO

Beside me the tall man laid his hands on a wire of the bridge, calmly, at rest. What they said was *nothing more.*

I didn't think I should wait for an ending which might or might not be mine. I knew that if it *was* mine it would follow or find me one way or the other. Where would not matter to it, or it would have it in mind. I wanted to see Jawbones Hill again and look for sheep.

I said: "I will go back to the surface. I've made up my mind."

"A good choice," the man nodded, as if I'd had many to chose from.

"Where will you go?"

He shrugged as if there was only one answer and he was quite happy with that. His hands said *I will go on. It's for the best.*

"I'm pleased to have met you," I told him, because I wanted to be polite.

"Likewise," he said. "Goodbye, Issy." *Farvæl.*

MAROONED

I do not know how long it took me to return to the top of the tower in the sea, but when I got there I was alone. There was no Patrice, no Aüggie, no tall man, no sense of an ending. When I looked out of a porthole there was no *Sweet Amelia* either.

I was sad that *Sweet Amelia* was gone becasue I had grown fond of her, despite her many flaws. Now I wondered if I was marooned, here in the tower beside the well in the ocean.

It didn't feel wrong if I was, but neither did it feel entirely right, either. I wondered if my sense of an ending had been wrong. Or perhaps this *was* the end and I could not see it because now it was hovering directly over my head like a small cloud, out of sight, like a hat.

When it grew dark I thought I would sleep on it and see what that brought. So that's what I did.

In the morning the tide had brought *Sweet Amelia* back, nuzzling at the side of the tower as if she was pleased to have found her way home after a somewhat ill-advised venture.

Before she could decide to go adventuring again I thought I had better take advantage of the situation. Aüggie still wasn't there so I left him a note before I climbed down the 33 rungs of the ladder. It said:

"*Goodbye, Aüggie, love Issy.*

PS: Sweet Amelia *came back. I did not swim away.*"

NOT END/END NOT

HARD TO SAY

It is hard to say how long I have lived with Sam Hall in the wooden house beside his garden.

It has been a fair time.

Because this is Hallows is-Land Sam Hall grew older. Then old. Mellowed. Yellowed like the apples in the sun. Wrinkled, browned; grew in sweet-scentedness; finally laid in the deep-tilled black earth of his garden. I have an ache in my back and dirt in the fine lines and cracks of my hands from the digging.

Now I sit on the steel riveted plates of the porch and look out across the garden in the evening sunshine. I drink sloeberry hooch – just a little – and miss Sam Hall's stick-like body in his dungarees.

But this is the way of it on Hallows. We all know. Even Sam.

My, my, he would say if he was sitting beside me and I had said those thoughts aloud to him. *All of that? My, my.*

Tomorrow I will leave. On Hallows the decay will begin to take hold. I can already feel it.

GONE

The Town is very quiet these days. The Siisters have Gone. Per si-Lversum and Charlie, Not-Mr Meyer are Gone. Nancé remains and she is like a broken doll.

There has not been an Exchange & Mart Day for almost as long as anyone can remember. Most of the people who used to live in the Town moved away and it is too far for them to come back to be marters. I think the things that happened here in the Square after the Tea Dance may still be too painful for them.

Of course, the Flying Horse Tea Room has never re-opened. When I return to the very tall house near the square the gate snaps at my fingers. I had forgotten. I turn away.

And then I turn back, to use the front door.

Inside I climb the 77 stairs. Past the stain on stair 76/64, back to my room.

I remember things I have forgotten. That is why I am here.

THE PICNIC ON HUISH

I have the picnic laid out on a plaid rug in the dunes, although the breeze blows sand grains across it. I keep the egg sandwiches in a tin so they will not become gritty. The Tea Room chickens have gone wild but still produce eggs of sky blue if you know where to find them.

I wait for a while, until my feet and the hem of my skirt have dried. When they have a girl comes along the beach, into view between the dunes. She is paddling at the water's edge and pauses to pick up a shell. When she discards it she sees me, sitting on the picnic rug beside the hamper. She comes to speak with me.

"Hello, Issy," I say.

"I didn't know anyone was here," she tells me. "Only Patrice and myself – that's what I thought. Have you just Arrived?"

"In a manner of speaking," I tell her. "But not as you mean."

I invite her to sit and we talk for a while. Then she eats an egg sandwich and drinks a glass of cordial before confessing herself tired. She lays down on the rug and covers her eyes with her forearm, although she continues to talk, telling me this and that. In the end the only thing I say is "You must go."

"Are you sure?"

I tell her that I am. It's for the best. When she hears this she seems convinced.

"Take something with you," I say. "You forgot it last time."

I hand her the polished cube of a box with solid brass hinges. She thanks me and smiles politely.

A little while later I watch them sail away – in a manner of speaking – for there is no sail, only oars.

"HELLO, ISSY"

When they are lost from my view to the distance I walk to the other end of Huish, where – near sunset – I have a view of a beach on Whelme, across the water, and so watch the Arrival of a man and his wife who is heavily pregnant. It is too far to see well, but I think I recognise Charlie, Not Yet-Mr Meyer, Poll Smiles and Francis Daychild (just the one). There is someone else there but I can't tell who they are.

I watch as the man in the boat hands a seaman's kitbag to Francis and a small suitcase to Charlie. He helps his wife to step out of the boat and into the calf-deep water, then he leads her to land.

His wife has taken two steps on the sand when she drops to her knees. The baby is coming. Of course.

Hello, Issy, I think.

WAIT, ONE AND TWO

There are two kinds of waiting – or three if you count waiting in the Waiting Room to visit Fryst is-Land. But I don't. It would only confuse matters.

Waiting of the first kind is the kind of waiting you must do because you know what to do when the waiting is over: when the correct moment arrives.

All my time with Sam Hall was a waiting of this kind. All that time, woven and spent in the flower beds and turning the dark earth; sipping sloeberry hooch; chasing squirrels; loving Sam.

But now that first kind of waiting is over because I have done what I was waiting to do; with egg sandwiches, a plaid picnic blanket and a thing forgotten/remembered.

Waiting of the second kind is waiting because you do not know what is coming next, or next next after next. You do not know what to do when it arrives, even if you recognise it, which you may not. You may wait and wait and nothing may arrive at all. You don't know.

I don't know for what I am waiting. I only know that I am. I don't know what comes next so I know my waiting is of the second kind and there is only one place that is best to do this, so I go there.

NEXT

I wait on the waiting bench by the harbour for as long as my arm, then longer. Just waiting. I don't know what comes next. And then I do.

RESIDUUM

I hear a flittering soft chatter in the air, somewhere near. I know what it is. As I sit up – because I have been lying down on the bench with my forearm over my eyes – the metanism alights on the bench. Worn out, poor thing. Exhausted. It alights, folds its wings, becomes still.

I am looking at its stillness, it's tarnished metals, when I hear a faint *toot-toot* of a steam whistle.

I look out to sea, beyond the harbour's Ω walls. I see the boats.

It's a flotilla, under chicken egg-blue sky; glitter-glistening across the water. There are so many I can't count them. (Patrice could, I know.)

"We are here," they are saying in their bunting and flags; in the chugging steam from their boilers and the smoke from their fire boxes; in the snapping of sail-ends caught by the breeze.

They are here and it's *dandy*.

Printed in Great Britain
by Amazon